Christmas Serenade

Cheryl Wright

CHRISTMAS SERENADE

Cover Artist: Black Widow Books

Copyright 2019 by Cheryl Wright

Small Town Romance Publications

Dedication

To Margaret Tanner, my very dear friend and fellow author, for her enduring encouragement and friendship.

To Alan, my husband of almost fifty years, who has been a relentless supporter of my writing and dreams for many years.

To Virginia McKevitt, cover artist and friend, who always creates the most amazing covers for my books.

To You, my wonderful readers, who encourage me to continue writing these stories. It is such a joy knowing so many of you enjoy reading my stories as much as I love writing them for you.

Table of Contents

Her pace quickened. It was just around the corner now, and she turned her head again. Silence reigned.

Of course her imagination was playing games with her.

Despite that, Felicity was incredibly relieved when she arrived into the safety of George's eclectic delicatessen and breathed in the mix of wonderful aromas. Coffee, muffins, homemade cakes – all familiar and comforting scents.

She was shaking and felt sure she must be white as a ghost. She'd been going there so long, she was sure George would notice something amiss, so tried to keep her voice steady.

"Hello, George," she said, planting a fake smile on her face. "It's a lovely night."

George frowned. "What's up? You don't look so good." He stared into her eyes, daring her to tell a lie.

Felicity shrugged. "Nah, I'm okay. Just a little tired." She hoped it would be enough to get him off her back, but he could be difficult to fool. "Can I have one of your yummy fruit muffins, please?" She reached for her purse. "Oh, and a coffee too. A *big* one!"

George frowned again but began to fill her order. "Yeah, sure. Take a seat, Felicity. I'll bring it over."

She sat fiddling with her hands until her order arrived. George placed the items on the table, as well as a coffee for himself, then sat opposite

Felicity. She looked around. The deli was near empty. It was just the two of them.

She swallowed. Here it comes, she thought.

George had owned the deli for as long as Felicity could remember – it had been her favourite haunt for years.

George was more than a deli owner to her, he was a very dear friend.

She picked up her coffee and began to sip it, ignoring George's presence, as though ignoring him would make him go away.

"Felicity," he demanded. "Tell me what's going on."

She stared at him, knowing she could never hide the truth from this dear man.

"Going on?" she said it a squeaky, uneven voice, then swiped at her face with the back of her hand. "I was followed here, that's what. Down the little alleyway." There, she'd said it, and there was no taking it back.

He stared at her intensely. Looked directly at her shaking hands, then scrutinised her face, taking in every feature, studying every movement.

"Then you're not walking home alone." With that he stood, and took off his apron, then locked the door. There was no arguing. He'd made up his mind it was clear. And Felicity knew better than to try and dissuade George. It had never worked in the past.

He sat once again, sipping his coffee, patiently waiting until she was ready to leave.

* * *

Hector Montgomery paced the floor, his anger rising with every step. What the heck was wrong with his daughter? "No, no, no!" he shouted. "Don't look at the ground, keep your head high!"

He'd had just about enough of her ingratitude and selfishness. After all the years he'd put into her career, and she repaid him like this? Downgraded him from manager to what? Nothing more than a lackey. *How dare she!*

After all his sacrifices, the wheeling and dealing, and now, with stardom and enormous wealth within his grasp, she was acting like some two-bit prima donna. He wouldn't stand for it. She *would* obey him or face the consequences! And, he would find a way to get her money, that was certain.

He should never have gotten mixed up with Fiorelli and his equally vicious cronies, wouldn't be so desperate for funds if he had kept away from them. The big money, this deal he was working on, would clear all his debt and still leave plenty over to spend.

Damn Felicity and her tantrums. Sex sold, it was a well-known fact. It wasn't as if he was asking her to prostitute herself.

"You're supposed to ooze sex appeal." He slapped his forehead. "What is this, this…?"

"I don't want to be a Pop Princess; I don't want to be the next Madonna!" Felicity stomped her foot as she always did when she didn't get her own way.

She was acting like a spoiled teenager, Hector decided. She'd been like this for years, since she was three. No matter how much he tried, he was never able to get her out of that foot-stomping habit of hers.

Regardless, he *was* trying to turn her into the next Madonna, but she constantly resisted. What was wrong with her?

"Felicity!" Hector's harsh voice reverberated through the room. "Sex kitten? Now?"

Hector watched as Felicity closed her eyes and took a deep breath. "Yes, Father," she said.

He smiled shrewdly at her meek acquiesce. He *would* get his own way. Eventually. He always did.

Chapter Two

Smoke hit Derek St James in the face as he glanced around, and the smell of booze and cheap cigars assaulted his senses.

This was not where he wanted to be.

He watched a waitress flirt with customers, openly rubbing her bare legs against customer's legs, hips, even hands. He averted his eyes at the sickening scene, nearly gagging as a tray of food passed him by. The smell of greasy, fat-ridden hamburgers churning his stomach to a point of almost retching.

As he walked toward an empty table he almost slipped on a piece of lettuce carelessly discarded and left to rot. A customer who'd had more than his fill of alcohol bumped into Derek, spilling beer over his well-kept suit.

As he brushed the liquid away, the full impact of where he was hit him, and he wondered how safe it was, and wanted desperately to leave. But he was here for a reason; he couldn't leave yet.

The music began as he neared the bar. His heart beating faster, Derek turned his head toward the stage in anticipation. He'd listened to the demo tape, sent to him by someone who was sure he'd be interested in this songbird. But now he'd seen the flea-bitten joint where she worked, he wasn't so sure.

The incessant chatter suddenly stopped as she began to sing. Her voice was strong, clear.

Felicity exposed her soul with each and every word she sang.

He pushed through the crowd, past the occupied tables and toward the only empty spot left - in the corner of the room.

He listened, mesmerised by her voice, the sincerity, the purity of the soulful words. The demo tape was raw, obviously an amateur recording, and went nowhere near the real thing. He closed his eyes, wanting to fully appreciate this rare talent. He drank in her voice and the vibes it created.

He opened his eyes with a jolt as the crowd began to applaud, whistling and chanting for more.

She gracefully bowed and began to back away, heading for the stage door. Her eyes scanned the room as she did so, and he stood.

It was at that moment their eyes met.

* * *

Felicity hated that she had to sing in this sleazy dive.

It was the lowest of the low. She had never envisioned herself performing in a place like this. But it was also the only place she got to sing what she wanted to sing, and not what everyone else wanted. *What her father wanted*, she thought bitterly.

Most of the time she was a reluctant Madonna wannabe and that didn't sit well with her. Her parents had carefully moulded her career over many years. Singing lessons, dance lessons, and classes on deportment.

When she'd looked back over her childhood, she realised she didn't have one. She'd spent almost her entire life living her parents dream.

Their dream, not hers.

It was *their* dream to have her perform at the age of four. The cute little girl who enhanced their pitiful act. Without her no one would have ever hired them. She was the drawcard. Had been for as long as she could remember. Not that she saw any real benefit from all her work. They stole every cent she'd ever earned. She should have been rolling in money, but instead she was barely breaking even.

Felicity swallowed back a sob. Now was not the time to wallow in the past. Tonight was all about her future. A future of singing the Blues.

At twenty-five, she knew it was time to change. Past time to change. And if performing in this dump meant building toward her dream, so be it.

She glanced around at the applauding crowd as she backed away. Cheap drinks, cheap cigars, torn jeans and cheap clothes.

Rock bottom. She was at rock bottom.

As he stood she saw him – he had a smile on his face and was wearing an expensive suit.

She simply couldn't look away.

* * *

Derek knocked loudly on Felicity's dressing room door, which was more like a closet it was so tiny.

She popped her head around the door and he could see she was apprehensive. He thrust his business card into her hand before she had a chance to speak. "Derek St James," he said. "I want to be your manager."

She stood there open mouthed, watching his every move as he scanned every inch of her. He watched her reaction closely.

"I don't need a manager, but thanks anyway," Felicity said crossly as she started closing the door.

She didn't even give him a chance! He jammed his foot in the door, preventing her from shutting him out. "Can we at least talk about it?" He could see this wasn't going to be easy.

"No." The foot was a bad move, he decided. It only made her more annoyed.

"Remove your foot, or I'll call security," she said, scowling at him.

Taking a step back, he opened his mouth to speak, but she slammed the door, leaving him standing dumbfounded.

Damn! He was just as annoyed with himself as he was with her. He should have taken it easy, not gone like a bull at a red rag.

He knew the moment she opened her mouth – she was the next Patsy Cline. Or Billie Holiday. He had to convince her to sign with him; there was no way he was letting an opportunity like this slip through his fingers.

He lifted his hand and was ready to pound on the door until she opened it. He stopped mid-air, realising it was a bad idea. A very bad idea.

Shoulders sagging, with his back against the wall, Derek recalled the last time he'd done this. A shiver went down his spine. He'd been heavy handed with the last performer he'd represented, and look where that got him. He wasn't going to risk that again. It simply wasn't worth it. It wasn't his fault; he didn't force her to... He shook the bitter memories away.

"Come on Felicity, let me in," he said in a voice that was barely audible. Very unlike him.

He decided to reassess his actions. Perhaps he was being too forward, or too informal? At this point he was willing to try anything.

He recalled her face as she told him she didn't need a manager. She looked almost...terrified. *Why would that be?*

Why did it always have to be so difficult? Why were *they* so difficult? He knew from experience that performers like Felicity Montgomery had no idea how great they were, or how famous they could become. Would become.

He just wanted to talk, he really did. He thought again about her expression on opening the door. Totally petrified. Strange.

Without the makeup she wore on stage, Felicity was even more beautiful. In so many ways she reminded him of.... *No!* He mentally slapped himself. He wasn't going there.

The biggest problem he faced right now was actually talking to her. She seemed determined not to let him penetrate her armour.

She might have thought she'd won this round, but he wasn't one to give up so easily. He knew talent when he saw it and heard it, and this girl had real talent.

He decided to rethink his strategy and left the building.

As he sat out in the alleyway, waiting outside the stage entrance, he pondered the past. *Selena Alexander.* Where had he gone wrong? Was it really his fault? Any of it?

Her mother certainly thought so. She'd blamed him for everything. Still blamed him. He'd wanted nothing more than to see her name in lights. To see her credited for the star she was. To know he'd found *the one.*

He wasn't to know it would end in her death. *How could he?*

He could never have guessed the outcome. A shudder ran through him, but not from the cold of the night air. His thoughts were playing havoc with his heart. Guilt overwhelmed him.

He heard the door bang before he saw her. Felicity Montgomery. She stood in the shadows, the street light forming her silhouette. As he moved, her head shot up.

"Who's there?" She glanced about. "Is s-someone out there?" Her voice was barely above a whisper. A terrified whisper.

"It's Derek St James," he called back, trying not to startle her, although it appeared to be too late for that. "I just want to talk to you, Ms. Montgomery. Felicity."

He heard her sigh as the light breeze sent wisps of hair flying around her face. "I didn't mean to scare you," he called.

"You didn't," she said, but he wasn't convinced. "Was there something you wanted?" she asked, nervously looking around.

He stepped out of the shadows and shrugged his shoulders. "You wouldn't talk to me inside, so I decided to wait. I'll walk you to your car," he said. "It isn't safe to walk out alone this late. In this neighbourhood." In this sleazy neighbourhood, he'd wanted to say. He was sure she would understand the innuendo.

Felicity looked him up and down, much like she did inside, only this time more thoroughly. Perhaps she thought he didn't see her in the dim night light, but it was all perfectly clear. Even in the darkness.

"This is me," she said, as they arrived at a small car. She took a deep breath, as if finally coming to a decision. "I'll call your office tomorrow." She must have seen his doubt, or felt his doubt, because she hastily added, "Promise."

Moments later she was gone.

He stood and stared after her, wondering if he'd ever see her again. Hoping above all hopes that he would. Felicity was a star and could make it to the top with the right guidance. He'd done it before, and he would do it again. If only she would let him.

As Derek made his way back to his own car, he glanced around. This sure was a scary place.

He felt as though someone was watching him. Eyes probing him in the darkness. Except for the stray cats scrounging through the bins looking for food, there was dead silence. The eerie quiet put him on edge, and the hair on the back of his neck stood up.

He heard a dog bark, followed by several cats screeching, then silence again. That was when he heard it. Footsteps. Soft footsteps, like someone trying to conceal their presence.

Derek turned his head sharply and saw the silhouette of a man leaning against a car as though he was waiting for someone.

As he looked about, Derek noticed the glow of a cigarette end. It was unnerving. A shiver went through him as realisation dawned. If he hadn't been out here waiting for Felicity, what might have happened to her?

With no acknowledgement from the other man, Derek had no idea if he even realised someone else was there. "Evening," he said, ensuring the man was aware of his presence.

Strolling at a quicker than normal pace, Derek made his way back to his car.

* * *

Felicity wasn't sure why she'd called Derek St James, she'd never intended to, but she felt inexplicably drawn to him.

So here she was, two days later, in his office.

She scanned the room as she sat opposite him – a man in whom she would place a lot of trust, a man who could change her life forever.

Why did she have these feelings toward someone she'd only known for a matter of days? Was it the promise of a big career? He seemed so down-to-earth. Not the type of person who would lead her on or make false promises. But one never knew.

It's not like she'd heard of him before, because she hadn't. And she didn't even know who to ask, except perhaps her parents. But she barely spoke with them anymore. Whenever she did, their bitterness rubbed off on her. Their heart-ache only served to remind Felicity of her own failed relationship.

Mike Singleton. A name she never again wanted to hear. A face she never again wanted to see. A man....

Stop! She was panicking, and her thoughts were running away from her. She needed to take a deep breath and calm down. Felicity reminded herself where she was, and why she was there.

Derek St James, and his once-in-a-lifetime offer.

She'd just have to go by her gut feelings, and in this instance, she was pretty sure her gut was right in telling her to forge ahead.

"......one year." What did she miss?

"Uh, sorry. What did you say?" He would think her a pure scatterbrain.

"I was saying that we really need to allow several months to prepare for your big debut." His brown eyes met hers. It was almost as though he was trying to look inside her thoughts. "Okay. This is what I have in mind. Look it over, get your solicitor to check it out too...." He handed her a contract and she balked. It was too soon for decisions. Decisions that could completely change her life.

Sure, she wanted this, she needed it. Her career, her totally wrong career, was at a stand-still, and some days she felt as though she was peddling backwards instead of moving forward. Despite all her hard work, despite her father pushing her each and every day. Despite everything.

As she reached out to accept the wad of paper he offered, their hands touched. Briefly. Just long enough for the melding of skin to send a thrill up her arm.

Her head jerked up. *Did he feel that too?* His eyes told her he did, but she'd decided long ago to freeze out any efforts to thaw her heart. Her very broken and worn out, never to be opened again, heart.

She had vowed to never again risk getting close to a man, and she would be true to her word.

Felicity felt confused. Although this was what she wanted, she wasn't sure she could do it. Surely it was better not to try than to fail? And what about these unwanted feelings she was having toward Derek? That wouldn't help her career at all, but rather, it would complicate things.

She stood suddenly, thrusting the papers at him as though they burned her, her eyes brimming with tears. "I can't do this," she said in a shaky whisper, and bolted for the door before he even realised what had occurred.

What the heck......? Derek sat bewildered in her wake.

One minute they were discussing strategies and contracts, and the next she was gone. Still, he'd been through this very scenario before. Selena Alexander would have been a star – a very big star.

He shook himself. It was still too raw, and he couldn't put himself through all that pain and angst again. He had to move forward, to take life by the horns and get on with it.

Otherwise survival would be impossible.

Derek looked down at the pile of papers Felicity had shoved at him. What was her problem?

He thought over what had taken place.

She seemed fine when they'd talked, but then she drifted into oblivion. Something triggered the episode, but what? No, wait... That wasn't it at all. She'd reacted when he passed over the contract.

That moment was etched in his memory. You could almost say it was burned there. *Oh heck! Did she feel that too?*

Derek strolled over to the window and stared out. She was there, down on the pavement, pacing back and forth.

When she glanced up and saw him there, she stopped momentarily, then headed for the subway.

Chapter Three

He knew he would find her here. In this sleazy smoked-filled bar.

She'd avoided his calls and wouldn't answer the door. He was positive she knew it was him, but wouldn't let him in.

He still wasn't sure why she'd changed her mind, what had triggered her unpredictable reaction. But it was in her eyes. Her beautiful piercing blue eyes. Eyes that reached out and gazed into his soul.

She was on the verge of tears when she'd bolted. Strangely enough, he'd known it was coming. It had something to do with her total lack of concentration while he explained the process. The long, drawn out process of moulding a star. Or in Felicity's case, a super-star.

"And now, Miss Felicity Montgomery!" The MC announced Felicity's arrival on stage. Several patrons made a cursory glance her way, then returned to their drinks and conversations. How she was able to stand this lack of respect he had no idea.

He sat at the bar, his back to the stage, not able to bear the thought of her singing here.

The voice was unmistakable. It was 'his' Felicity. He slowly swivelled his chair around to face her. She glanced up, and he swore she looked directly at him.

Lifting his glass in a silent toast, she acknowledged him with a terse nod. She was so not happy he was here.

Oh, that angel's voice. He had to sign her, he just had to! This could be the most important move of his entire career. And her career.

Derek listened, mesmerised by the voice of the century. He closed his eyes, taking in the vibrations and the beat of the music, and the perfection of her performance.

Opening his eyes, he watched as the lights played against her long white dress. It was slinky, sexy, and the spotlights sent shimmering cascades of colour along the length of her body. Highlighting every curve. Sending his nerve endings into a spin.

He mentally slapped himself. Felicity was a potential client, and he needed to keep that in mind.

The sudden applause brought him out of his revelry and back to the present. A standing ovation. In a place like this? Surely this would be enough to convince her she needed to sign with him?

But Derek wasn't convinced. Although he'd met her only recently, he'd already had a taste of her stubbornness. It was not going to be easy getting her to sign that contract.

* * *

She sat rigid, her lips pursed into a tight line.

Just as he'd predicted, Felicity was being difficult. "Of course, you should have your solicitor look the contract over," he heard himself say. "This is a big step in your career."

Her eyes penetrated his. "Of course," she said. But she said it without conviction.

He'd already lost her.

He reached out and touched her shoulder. "I know how scary this must be for you," he said. "But we're in this together. I'll be there every step of the way."

She smiled. But it was only window dressing. Just something to appease him and get him the heck out of there.

She looked at the contract. It was a cursory glance – her eyes darted all over the place. First at the pages in her hand, then at him. Back to the paper, back to him. *What was she thinking?*

And what was he thinking, putting his hands on her? Last time they touched – skin to skin – a thrill shot up his arm and through his body.

"Okay," she folded the contract and placed it in her handbag. "I'll check it out and get back to you." With that she stood, effectively ending their meeting.

But he didn't want it to end. He felt good when he was with her. Life seemed to matter when she was around.

* * *

"And one, and two, and...." The choreographer was getting frustrated. Felicity could see it a mile off.

"Sorry Joe. Can we start over?" Her lack of concentration was messing everything up. She had a big show Saturday night, and still didn't know the routine well enough to perform.

"Okay everyone. Let's take ten." Joe walked toward Felicity, motioning for her to wait. "This isn't like you, Felicity. Come on, out with it."

Joe and Felicity had worked together for as long as she could remember. He was her mentor, her choreographer, and her best friend.

Shaking her head, she backed away. But he could see right through her. "It's a man! You've gone and got yourself a man. About time too!"

Joe made kissy sounds at her, as he fixed his disorganised hair. "Maurice!" Joe motioned for his long-time partner and Felicity's wardrobe manager to join them. "Our Felicity has got herself a man."

"Ooooh, you two!" Felicity knew they meant well, but they were always trying to match her up with *the perfect man.* It was soooo frustrating!

"I do not want to talk about it," she said. Then quickly added, "Anyway, you've got it all wrong. There is no-one." But it was too late. They saw through her.

"Yeah, right." The men spoke in unison, and grinned at each other, nodding their heads. They didn't believe a word she said.

Felicity sighed. "If you must know," she said quietly, "I've been approached by someone who wants to be my agent. But I'm going to say no. Now can we get back to work?"

"Are you crazy?"

"What are you thinking girl?"

She waved them away and headed to left stage, her starting point, leaving the flabbergasted men in her wake.

* * *

She looked incredibly alluring up on that big stage, dressed in her skimpy outfit, and backed by an impressive band.

Oh boy, she sure could wiggle that tiny butt.

Derek had gone to see Felicity in action. And he sure did like what he saw.

But he understood why this was not what she wanted. The skimpy outfits and lecherous men ogling her.

This was her bread and butter job. For now. He intended to turn that around.

Outstanding! The air was littered with electricity. The audience were on their feet, clapping, whistling, and yelling. They simply couldn't get enough of her.

Then the mood changed. The lights dimmed, and Felicity moved toward the edge of the stage, her microphone centimeters from her mouth, paused and waiting for the music.

The applause began again as she began to sing. They couldn't get enough of this incredibly talented performer. What on earth had she been thinking when she'd refused his offer? Derek was so grateful he'd call Joe, and the two of them had taken things into their own hands. Being the proactive guy he was, Joe had set up a meeting after tonight's show.

Not that Felicity had any idea, because she didn't. He hated to think what her reaction would be, but Joe knew what he was doing. He was a good friend to Felicity and would ensure she did the right thing to enhance her career.

At least Derek hoped he could.

Chapter Four

Derek sat nervously in Felicity's dressing room.

He wanted to arrive after her, making it almost impossible for flight, but Joe insisted she needed to see him and make her own decisions.

Fair enough.

Of course, devious as he was, Joe had said he'd block her way out, and Maurice would be on hand to help, so there was no risk involved anyway.

"Brilliant!" he heard Joe say. "Absolutely brilliant – the crowd loved you, as they always do." As the voices got ever closer, Derek became more and more nervous. He'd done this before, many times, so why the heck was he panicking over this?

Because this could change your entire life, he reminded himself.

Derek looked up as the door handle rattled. Sweat trickle down his face as the door opened. Felicity had a towel draped over her shoulders, and Joe had his arm around her.

She stopped dead when she spotted Derek, pulling her lips into a tight little ball. If looks could kill...

"It's not what you think, my darling," Joe said to Felicity, and then reneged. "Actually it is. This is what you've worked so hard to get, and now you're going to let it all fade away?" Joe pouted momentarily, then smiled. "Yes, it was a damned conspiracy! So sue me." He shrugged, grinned at Derek, and then backed off.

Felicity glanced from one to the other of the men. "Really, you two. This just isn't fair," she said as she plonked herself down on a chair. "It seems I don't have a choice, so say what you have to say, then leave," she told Derek.

Taking a deep breath, Derek pulled his chair closer to Felicity's and took her hand in his. Big mistake! A shiver overtook him. As he stared into Felicity's eyes, he knew she felt it too, but he had to push on, had to try and ignore it. After all, it was surely a result of anticipation – for both of them.

"I know you're scared, and I know what a bully Hector has been. I'm not like that." He waited for her reaction but got none so pushed on. "What I'm proposing is to mold your career – your Blues career. The singing career you want, not the one your parents mapped out for you."

He leaned back in his seat and waited, and waited, and waited. She didn't utter a sound for what seemed like hours but was only a matter of minutes. He could almost hear her mind churning over, weighing up the options, making her decision.

After all, this would be a life-changing decision. Her life would never be the same once he unleashed her onto an unsuspecting public.

"Ok—aay," she said. "But with conditions."

Derek's heart fluttered. She said okay? Okay!! He was in, he could feel the excitement rising up inside him. But he had to play it cool. He couldn't let her see how much this meant to him. It had to be all about her. His heart fluttered in anticipation.

"What sort of conditions are we talking about?" he said, trying to sound suspicious.

"To start with, I will only work with Joe and Maurice. We've been together for years."

Derek looked across at the grinning Joe. "No problem. Done." With his heart pounding in his head, he metaphorically rubbed his hands with glee. *Yes! This is really going to happen!*

Felicity licked her lips and stared right into his eyes. Uh-oh. "The next condition is totally not negotiable." He could feel the sweat dripping down his face. "My father cannot, under any circumstances, find out about this until I'm ready to tell him."

"But he's not your manager anymore," Maurice blurted out. "What does it matter?"

Felicity shrugged her shoulders and glared at Joe, then eye-balled Maurice who now stood at a safe distance behind Joe. "I am going to get rid of him altogether. But in my time," she said, determined.

Derek's gaze moved from one to the other of them. Joe and Maurice were nodding slightly, egging him to agree, but Derek wasn't sure he wanted to. Hector had contacts in the business. Lots of them. He could bring Derek down in the blink of an eye. He could also ruin Felicity's career before it even got off the ground.

It was a risk he knew he had to take. "No problem," he said, shaking her hand when he really wanted to pull her to him and hug her with all his might. "I'll have my solicitor draw up a new contract, and you'll have it in a couple of days." He pulled out his handkerchief and wiped the sweat from his face.

Standing, he watched Joe and Maurice, whose expressions mimicked his feeling of relief.

"And you two," she said, poking the two men in the chest, "Are in deep doo-doo. You planned this whole thing, didn't you?" Then she moved in and hugged them both. "Thank you," she whispered, tears brimming to the surface. "I love you both for seeing what an idiot I've been."

Derek took the opportunity to slip away quietly before she could change her mind. Whistling loudly, he almost skipped down the corridor on his way out of the building.

* * *

In an effort to keep his promise not to let Hector know what was going on, Derek hired an old warehouse on the other side of town. They didn't need a stage for rehearsals, but he would have to make some changes. At the very least they'd need a dressing room for Felicity, somewhere to store costumes, backdrops, and the list went on. He didn't care about the outlay, that was the least of his problems, but Hector was another story altogether.

Derek knew his career could be over in a flash if Hector found out and blacklisted him in the industry. Of course that was the worst possible scenario; surely Hector wouldn't go that far. Or would he? Derek honestly didn't know. But the man had a reputation for being ruthless when it came to his daughter's career.

What he did know was Felicity was about to become a star of the highest order.

"Morning!" She'd arrived for her first day of rehearsals. The first day of her new life.

"Good morning, Felicity." His whole day brightened just seeing her here.

He would keep things formal. He didn't want the attraction he felt for her to interfere with their business arrangement.

Before he knew what was happening, Felicity hugged him.

"You were right, this *is* what I want." With her arms around him, warmth seeped into him, but he didn't reciprocate. He wouldn't hug her back. *He wouldn't!*

But his body had a mind of its own, and before he could stop himself, his arms slipped up and around her. She melted into him as though they'd done this a thousand times before. He felt as though he'd come home, as though this was where he belonged – in her arms, with Felicity close to him.

He released a huge sigh before he could stop it. *Oh yeah, this was good. Maybe too good.*

Derek closed his eyes and enjoyed the moment. He could definitely get used to this. He took a deep breath and was rewarded with the wonderful fragrance that was Felicity. His moments of self-indulgence suddenly had a rude awakening.

"Oooooooooooh!" It a very delighted Joe.

"It's not what you think," Derek quickly said, pushing Felicity away. *What the heck was he thinking?* This was becoming far from a professional relationship and had to stop. Except he didn't want it to stop.

"Yes it is," Felicity said, clearly annoyed at Joe's inference. "I was giving Derek a thank you hug. And I'll thank you not to make a mountain out of a molehill." With that she stormed off to the other end of the warehouse, dropping her bags on one of the comfortable chairs Derek had purchased.

Joe shrugged, then grinned. "Okay, Sweets," he called after her. Then rubbing his hands together said to Derek. "Where is the sheet music, and where is Mr. Music? We can't start without him."

Oh no. Derek gave himself a metaphorical head slap. He'd forgotten the piano player. Reading his thoughts, Joe pulled out his phone and made a call. "On his way," he said after a few minutes.

"Coffee's here!" It was Maurice this time, totting several cups of steaming coffee. "Can't start the day without it." These guys thought of everything, and they were worth every cent, Derek realised.

The three men sat together drinking their coffee, discussing their plans. But Felicity chose to sit away from them as she wanted to absorb the words of the songs Derek had chosen for her.

Today was not about costumes, it was all about the quality of the performance. For the next few weeks they'd work on the words, getting the feel for the songs, learning how to pull at the heart strings of the audience, and getting it right.

The rest would come later. Much later.

* * *

Derek demanded a very high standard, and sometimes it was hard work, but Felicity was up to the task. She'd worked hard for her father all her life, nothing would change now.

But keeping her relationship with Derek professional was much harder.

Terrified Hector would find out she'd defected, Felicity kept conversations with him to a minimum. She still needed to attend rehearsals with him to avoid suspicion, which meant she was doing two different sets of rehearsals each week; for Derek, and for Hector.

It was exhausting.

But it was worth the added pressure and the effort. After all, this was her career at stake. Her dream, her life-long dream. To be the next Billie Holiday.

"Okay, Sweets," Joe called from across the room. "Show time!" He was exaggerating. Felicity had on her workout leotard – the one she used for rehearsals.

When he clapped his hands together impatiently, Felicity was startled, and quickly jumped from the chair. "Keep your pants on," she told him. "I'm coming!"

"Darling, do I have to?" Joe asked, a sly grin on his face. Felicity could feel her mood lifting. Joe knew how to get her up and functioning again, and in the mood for work.

"From the top please, Mr Music." Joe was so old fashioned, but Felicity didn't care. They'd worked together since she was a tot, and Joe understood her. He could read her without Felicity having to mutter so much as one word. And she could do the same with him.

Joe was like a male version of her fairy godmother. He looked out for her, and kept her on the straight and narrow. Protected her from her over-zealous parents on many occasions, when they'd pushed her too far.

As the music began, Felicity readied herself, doing some light stretches while she waited for her cue.

As she began to sing, Joe stood with a satisfied expression on his face, his finger on his chin. This was one of his favourites, Felicity knew it, and Derek knew it too. But it wasn't the opening song that Derek wanted. Open with a bang, he'd said.

With all the props in place, Felicity moved about the stage, rehearsing the moves Joe had choreographed, the routine almost down pat by now.

The words faded, and Felicity stood momentarily silent. She bowed as she would at the end of a performance. The slow clapping brought her attention to the back of the warehouse.

Her heart began to thunder in her chest as Derek walked slowly toward her. She gave herself a mental shake. Since when did she allow herself to react this way?

Since Derek St James stormed into your life, she answered silently. She didn't want to feel this way, didn't need the distraction.

Her life was complicated enough right now without the added challenge of a relationship. Especially a relationship with her agent. The man who could and probably would change her life forever.

"Excellent! Bravo!" he said, almost to the stage area by now.

"Thank you," Felicity said quietly, not sure if he really meant what he said.

"Ditto," Joe added, grinning broadly. "She's got the goods, all right." Embarrassed, Felicity turned away, heading toward her makeshift dressing room.

* * *

Rehearsing for both Derek and Hector was exhausting, and Felicity decided it couldn't continue any longer.

At her rehearsal with Hector that day, she pulled him aside. "Father. Hector," she said, determination in her voice. "We need to talk."

He stared into her face, no doubt trying to read it. But she kept her expression as blank as she possibly could.

"We've had our differences over the years," she said. "And I know you've always tried to do what's best for me…" It was a lie. Hector only thought about Hector, it was never about her. Never had been, and probably never would be.

His feet shifted from one to the other, as though he had an inkling of what was to come. "Just say it, Felicity," he growled. "What's going on?"

She saw the ferocious look on his face and nearly backed down but was determined to hold her ground. "I'm sorry, but your services are no longer required." The words spewed out much faster than she'd intended, but at least now they were out. "I have an agent now, he's looking after me." It was hard, but not as hard as she'd expected. Perhaps because it was something she should have done years ago.

"You ungrateful cow! I've worked hard all my life for you, got you where you are today!" He almost screamed the words at her, getting closer to her face with each word.

Then he paced the floor, arms flying all over the place, ranting and raving as he stomped around. Felicity tuned out and almost laughed out loud watching his crazy antics. She was determined not to cringe or let him see her fear, and just stood back with her arms crossed. She saw Joe peek out from behind the stage curtains, but apparently Hector hadn't as he said nothing about it.

About four minutes later she'd had enough.

"Goodbye Father," she said, thrusting an envelope toward him. "Here's a small severance to see you through."

Hector grabbed the envelope and stormed out. Felicity knew he would never knock back a chance at free money, no matter how small.

Maurice and Joe came out from behind the curtains. She didn't want to be alone with Hector when she told him and was very grateful for the back-up.

"It's over now, Sweets," Joe said, putting his arms around her. "You don't have to worry about him any more."

Felicity let out a huge sigh as she felt tears of relief trickle down her face.

* * *

Derek wondered if Felicity felt the same way he did. If her heart fluttered when he walked in the room?

It was crazy, this feeling he got when she was around. He couldn't allow it to continue; he simply couldn't afford to fall in love with a client.

Joe tossed him a towel and he followed Felicity into her dressing room, grabbing a cold bottle of water from the refrigerator on his way.

"Come in," she called, as he knocked gently.

His heart jumped a beat or two when she smiled at him. *What was that about?*

He loved the way her face shined after a performance. Sweat on anyone else was unbecoming, but on Felicity it was…sexy.

He watched as she drank the water, the way it trickled down her neck, the way her muscles flickered as the cold water hit her skin.

Then their eyes met. It was like they were on the exact same wave-length, as though their souls entwined. Felicity brought the water away from her mouth and licked her lips.

It was almost his undoing. Derek stepped forward and took the water from her hands and moved in to her. As Felicity's arms wrapped around him, it was as though something overtook him, as though he could no longer control what his body did. Derek felt himself move toward her mouth. His hands slowly slid up her neck, bringing her hair up too. He loved the silky feel of it, and the way it swung around her face when she danced.

As they came together, Felicity sank into him.

A tiny shiver went through his body, and as their lips met, he felt warmth, despite the cold water she'd been drinking. More than anything, he felt comfort. Love.

He mentally shook himself.

Not love, it was simply infatuation. That's what happens when you work closely with an attractive woman.

He reminded himself it wasn't that way with Selena, his former client. It was strictly business with her.

Felicity returned his kiss, and he could feel her heart beating wildly against his chest. It was then he realised she felt the same way he did. He was elated.

But where did they go to from here?

Chapter Four

Leading a double life had been difficult.

Felicity knew it would be, but she never for a moment dreamed it would be as hard as it was. Hiding her relationship with Derek, and more importantly, her hard work and efforts toward following in the footsteps of Billie Holiday was probably the hardest thing she'd done to date.

She was so glad it was all out in the open with Hector now. All her other commitments were now fulfilled, and she could just commit herself to Derek's rehearsals and plans for her.

Her parents had begun to groom her from the time she could walk. Felicity now questioned their motives. Was it for her benefit, or was it more personal? After all, as a child star, they received all money she earned. Instead of putting it away in a trust fund for her as they were meant to do, they had lavished gifts on her. Bought luxury cars and a house, clothes and more – for themselves. All for her benefit, of course.

Of course, she thought dryly. The taste of bitterness overwhelmed her.

What did she see of all that money in her adulthood? Not one cent. There was nothing to show for all her years of hard work. Except that was, for her parent's house, her parent's cars, and the holidays her parents took her on. All funded by Felicity.

She had every right to sue them for all the money they wasted, the houses, the cars and so-called gifts.

She reminded herself she was a professional performer now. She had to give them that. Without her parent's dedication, she wouldn't be working with Derek now.

They could keep it all. She didn't need all those things.

But it cut deep. If they'd done the right thing by her, she would be financially in a great position now. She wouldn't have been working in skimpy clothing all these years. But finally, it was over. Her new life had begun.

"A penny for them." It was Joe, doing his usual rounds and checking up on her.

Felicity sat in her dressing room, sweat pouring down her face from yet another rehearsal session, a towel wrapped around her shoulders.

She blinked, trying hard to keep threatening tears at bay.

"What's this then," Joe asked as he approached. He knew her too well; Felicity couldn't hide anything from him.

Her thoughts had taken her to a place she didn't want to be. "I was just thinking about all that money I earned as a child," she said quietly. "And how much my parents squandered." She glanced up at Joe. "And stole."

He opened his mouth to speak but didn't say anything.

"Joe?" She knew him well too. Whatever he wanted to tell her was on the tip of his tongue, but he hesitated. She wondered why.

He looked straight into her eyes, rubbed his hand across his chin. Pondering. Deciding whether or not to tell her something?

He shook his head, then straightened his shoulders. "Water under the bridge, Sweets," he told her, but his expression told her much more than his words ever would. He was holding something back, she was convinced of it. "This is your big opportunity. Don't let their selfishness spoil your big chance."

He was right of course. He always was. Still, Felicity wondered what it was he'd wanted to say but felt he couldn't. Maybe he simply agreed with her.

"Hugs." He opened his arms to her, and she accepted the invitation. "I know I'm not Derek, but I'm here for you, Sweets. Don't let your parents drag you down yet again."

Joe had been there for her forever. He understood her, always would. Felicity thanked her lucky stars for the day he'd come into her life.

* * *

It had been a hard day of rehearsing. Felicity was exhausted.

"Enough." Derek told her he was worried about her state of health. Long hours of rehearsing was taking its toll.

She nodded enthusiastically. Felicity was beyond exhausted and was definitely ready to hit the road. She would indulge in a night of veg'ing out, followed by a wonderfully deep sleep. That was the plan anyway.

She trudged toward her dressing room, towel around her shoulders.

She checked her phone. Five messages. *What could be so urgent?* Deep down she knew. Nothing was urgent, it never was. It was him again. Or was it a her?

As she listened to the playback, she felt dismayed. These anonymous messages were becoming menacing, more frightening. She had no idea who was ringing. Or what their intention was.

They never spoke, never said so much as a single word, but heavy breathing in the background was intimidating.

She heard a soft tap on the door. "Yes?" She hoped the distress she felt did not come across in her voice.

"Need a lift…?" Joe began but stopped mid-sentence. "What's wrong, Sweets?"

Trust Joe, he didn't miss a trick.

Should she tell him about the phone calls? About the feeling of being followed? Of being watched?

She shivered. No, it had to be her imagination. Okay, not the phone calls, but surely no one was following her, or watching her. Why would they?

Felicity stared directly into Joe's eyes. She hated lying to him, but she had to. He looked so worried right now.

"I'm fine. Just tired," she said, hating herself for deceiving her best friend.

"Or maybe you just need a hug." Joe wrapped his arms around her, not worrying about her sweaty body. Just wanting to wrap her up in his love.

She leaned into him, soaking up the love and support he provided. She could always trust Joe. There was no two ways about it, he would protect her from whatever happened. Or might happen.

But she didn't want to worry him, and worry he would.

"Thanks, Joe," she whispered, holding back tears. "I needed that."

"I know, Sweets. I always know," he whispered back. And that was exactly what Felicity was afraid of.

* * *

"We're going to practice some new dance steps today." Joe always looked for ways to enhance Felicity's performances.

It was really about the voice, but these days audiences expected more of an artist than just standing on the stage.

She could do it, no doubt about it. Felicity had been performing since she was a tiny tot, and had grown up being choreographed by Joe.

This was the least fun part of her act, but she knew it had to be done.

"Imagine the props in the background," Joe said. "There will be a staircase over there," he said, pointing to stage right. "You will make your entrance from there."

Stairs were the bane of Felicity's life. She always worried about slipping as she descended the steps. "Really? Stairs?" she asked in exasperation.

"I know, Sweets. You hate stairs, but you need a grand entrance. You are a star!" Joe said with a flourish.

Felicity pouted, hoping it would persuade him.

"Not working, Sweets. Put on your happy face instead." Joe smiled, and she laughed.

There was once a time that Felicity could wrap him around her little finger, but not anymore. He wanted this for her as much as she wanted it. And he was determined she would get there.

"Okay. Imaginary stairs. Look at them." He again pointed to stage right. "They will be spiralling out across the stage, but they won't be steep."

"So my costume won't interfere," she asked, already knowing the answer.

Joe frowned. "Come on, Sweets. You know the drill. Beautiful long flowing dress, high heels." He did a little spin wearing his imaginary full-flowing skirt. Felicity laughed out loud.

"Okay. You win."

Joe rubbed his hands together. "Wonderful. Now hold my hand and we'll practice the steps together."

Felicity and Joe had been practicing the new dance steps for most of the morning, but she needed to stop and catch her breath, so they took a break.

She sat on a stool in the middle of the imaginary stage while Joe talked to her about some changes he wanted to make.

Something caught her attention, and Felicity stared, trying to get a better glimpse.

She stretched her back and turned her neck toward the window.

"Felicity?" She barely registered he was talking to her. He turned his head and followed her line of view. "What's out there?"

She shook her head, trying to chase the vision away. "Not sure. I thought I saw someone at the window. Watching us." She flung her hands across in front of her, hoping to brush Joe's attention in another direction. "Obviously not. Never mind. What were you saying?"

As much as she'd tried to dismiss it, the expression on Joe's face told her he was more than a little concerned.

Chapter Five

Derek came up behind Felicity and slowly put his arms around her. A thrill went through her as it did every time he touched her.

Her heartbeat sped up, and she felt a little flutter low down in her belly, anticipating what might come.

He turned her around to face him, and gazed down into her face, his eyes staring at her rich red lips. Her tongue darted out to hydrate her parched lips. She'd wanted this, needed this, for far too long.

Unconsciously, she reached up and caressed his face with her fingertips. Softly, unhurriedly.

He leaned into her but stopped when his lips were only a whisper away from hers. Poised, ready to move, but waiting for her silent permission.

She sucked in a breath and closed her eyes, moving closer still.

He moved ever so slightly, and his lips touched hers, sending a shiver of pleasure through her entire body. It felt like tiny fairies dancing across her lips, their dance of love warming her whole being. Her arms went up around him, pushing her closer still. She felt his heartbeat against her chest, beating in time with hers.

A sigh left her lips; she was in heaven. She didn't want this moment to stop. Not now, not ever.

But stop it must. They were professionals working toward a common goal. They couldn't get involved. Not now. Not ever.

Felicity sighed, then pushed Derek away. He was confused, his expression said it all.

"I…" She was going to explain but clamped her lips together almost immediately. He understood, she was certain he did.

His eyes pierced her existence. Watching, staring, and penetrating her being. She tried to snatch her gaze from his but couldn't. They were meant to be, she was certain they were, but not like this. Not now. Not in this place and time.

She fought back tears knowing it may never be the right place or time. Knowing they may never be together. Realising her heart may forever be split in two, yearning for a man that she simply couldn't have.

Unable to face him any longer, she turned away to stare out the window, to contemplate her next move. How could she be happy without Derek at her side?

Her breath caught in her throat as she saw a blur. Was she being watched? Or was it her imagination? Her confusion was deepening instead of things falling into place.

She spun toward Derek. "Did you……?" She bit her lip. He'd think her an idiot.

He waited for her to finish the sentence, but no more words came. Instead Derek finished it for her. "Want to go to lunch? Sure, let's go." Derek grabbed her hand before she could protest and headed toward the door.

* * *

It was hard going home alone. More than ever, Felicity wanted to be with Derek. She sighed, knowing it could never be. They could never be.

Closing the door behind her, and ensuring it was locked, Felicity headed toward the bathroom. Todays rehearsals had worked up a sweat, and if there was one thing she truly hated, it was being able to smell her own body odour.

The water was warm and inviting. Felicity revelled in the comfort she derived from this small act of self-indulgence. Letting the warm water flow over her body, she leaned against the glass wall and let out the breath she didn't know she was holding. It felt good.

She hadn't felt this content for a long time. Since she suspected she was being followed. Was being watched. She wondered if her little apartment was even safe these days. More than once she'd come home to the feeling someone had been inside while she was gone.

A book out of place here, a cushion moved there. Just little things, but enough to raise her concerns.

For a time, she checked the unit the minute she walked in the door. But Felicity felt she was becoming paranoid, so stopped. Now she simply accepted that her apartment had to be secure.

It was after all her home. Her haven.

As she turned off the water, she stopped dead. There it was – a muffled sound. In her apartment.

She held her breath. They had to know she was here. They would have heard the running water, so she wondered how safe she was.

With the white fluffy towel wrapped around her, she inched her way out of the bathroom. Her bare feet made no sound.

She felt eyes on her, and braced herself for whatever may happen, standing still, all the while searching the room.

Something touched her feet and she let out a squeal. Thank goodness it was only her sweet little kitty, and not an intruder.

"Oh my gosh, you scared the heck out of me." She knelt to pat Meow. The kitty rubbed her head against Felicity's still-wet feet, encouraging her to pat her little head. That was when she heard the distinct click of the front door closing.

Felicity gasped.

Someone *had* been in her apartment. *Oh my gosh.*

Not knowing what to do next, and feeling extremely panicked now, she ran around and locked all the windows and closed all the blinds.

Tomorrow she would get new locks.

* * *

In the dead of the night, the telephone rang.

Felicity reached out for the handset, despite her dazed state of mind. "Hello?"

It would be the catalyst for the rest of the day, despite the caller only saying a few words. "I'm watching you." The words were said in a whisper, but with sinister intent behind them.

Felicity sat bolt upright in the pitch black of night. "Who is this?" The caller didn't respond. Heavy breathing was followed by deadly silence.

"What do you want?" She was screaming down the phone now. Bad enough when he rang her over and over but didn't say a word. This time it was a definite threat.

With her heart beating out of control, she froze with the handset to her ear. She heard a sound in the darkness. Was someone in the house? Was she still alone?

She had no idea. To appease her concerns, she flicked the light on, but the sudden brightness caused her to close her eyes tightly.

As she opened them, movement out of the corner of her eye made her gasp and hold her breath.

"Reow." Meow curled up beside her on the bed and began to knead, making himself comfortable.

"Oh, Meow, you scared me." Holding her hand to her heart, Felicity suddenly realised she still had the phone in her hand, and quickly replaced it.

She scrutinised the room. Were they watching her? Was she safe here? Gingerly climbing out of bed she pulled the curtains back, checked the windows were locked. Satisfied, she pulled the curtains back into their closed position and ensured no one could see inside.

She draped her robe around herself and moved into the lounge room, checking the windows, then checked the doors were secure. Then she double-checked them all again.

She'd not long finished when the phone rang again. This time she hesitated, knowing it was probably him again.

Felicity picked up the handset but didn't speak. "Just because your curtains are closed doesn't mean I can't see you." He chuckled, then disconnected the call.

For all of thirty seconds Felicity stood frozen in terror. Then she called the police.

* * *

When the knock came on the door, Felicity jumped. "It's the police," came a deep male voice. She looked through the peep-hole and sure enough, two police officers stood outside. "Can you hold up your ID please," she called out.

Certain these were real police, she opened the door, pulling her robe tightly around herself while trying to contain Meow at the same time.

She held the door opened while the two officers entered, and noticed two police cars outside. "Two officers are checking the parameter," the officer in charge explained. "If anyone is still here, we'll find them."

Felicity nodded her acknowledgement, almost too afraid to speak in case she broke down. She wasn't the sort of person to lose her cool easily, but this whole business had her on edge.

The second officer searched through her unit, making sure no one was in there with her. "I live alone," she told him.

"Just a precaution Ma'am," the officer said. "I'm checking that no one is hiding in here."

Felicity stumbled backwards. She hadn't considered that option at all. She'd always felt safe in her little apartment. She was surrounded by good neighbours, but still had her privacy and her independence.

Now she was at great risk of losing both. The officer helped her to the sofa, realising she was in shock. Felicity put her hands to her face and quietly sobbed.

The police were amazing. Professional but compassionate at the same time. They waited until she composed herself again before interviewing her.

"How long has this been going on?" one officer asked.

She had to admit it had started some time ago. *Perhaps a few months?*

"And nothing else has occurred out of the ordinary?" he wanted to know, all the time scribbling notes in his little black book. He looked up at her, waiting in anticipation.

"Well… I've had phone calls, and once or twice I was sure I was being followed." She took a deep breath. "But I couldn't see anyone. Then just the other day I was certain someone was watching me at rehearsals. Through the window."

"And you're just reporting this now? Don't you understand how serious this could be?" the second officer said, a disapproving expression on his face.

"I, I'm sorry. I didn't know what to do," she told him.

He reached over and patted her hand. "Well now we know, and we'll look into it. First off the rank is a trace on your phone. Write your number down for me and I'll set that up right now."

Felicity immediately felt better, but it didn't mean the problem would be resolved. Far from it.

While they spoke, the other officer was still wandering around the apartment. "Hey Pete," he called to the policeman talking to Felicity. "Check this out."

"Well I'll be…" Pete said, obviously surprised.

Felicity sat on the sofa, perplexed, but also worried. "What is it," she asked, not sure she really wanted to know.

"It's a small camera," Pete said. "You're being watched from inside your apartment."

* * *

Taking a gulp of cold water as she left her dressing room, Felicity walked toward Joe. But her eyes were not on him, they were focused on the windows. Correction. She was looking out onto the street. Her eyes moving toward each window, scanning each one individually.

Joe peered toward the window, squinting in an effort to get a better look. *What was out there?* Although *who* was out there was probably closer to the mark.

Felicity had been distracted for weeks. Her confidence seemed to be slipping, but it was more than that, he was certain.

He'd seen her glance over her shoulder on many occasions recently. And he'd seen the startled looks when someone moved quietly toward her.

And he sure as heck hadn't missed her panicked expression when her phone rang. *What was going on?*

This was not the Felicity he knew. She'd never been the type to scare easily. She was a strong-willed, strong-minded woman who knew what she wanted and went after it.

These days Felicity was jittery, frazzled. And more than a little skittish.

This was nothing like *his* Felicity. She had never acted like a scared little rabbit in her life. *Why was she doing it now?*

Joe took a deep breath and turned toward Felicity, to ready her for their last practice dance for the day.

A shiver went through him as he sensed someone watching him. He quickly turned back toward the uncovered window. That was when he saw it. The silhouette of a man watching them.

In the blink of an eye he was gone.

He turned and briskly grabbed Felicity by the shoulders. "What are you not telling me," he asked, his voice serious. "What are you hiding, Sweets," he demanded in the softest voice he could muster.

She stared directly into his eyes and lied. She'd never lied to him before all of this, and this revelation had him reeling. "What do you mean? I'm not hiding anything. I told you about the break-in the other night."

Did she honestly think she could keep something like this from him? He was a patient man, and he was certain Felicity would be scared, so he'd allow her this misdemeanor.

He stepped forward and pulled her into a big bear hug. Hugs could solve anything. But perhaps this time, that would be overstepping the expectation.

Joe felt Felicity shiver in his arms, felt her entire body shake. "Joe?" Her voice was soft, only a smidge above audible.

"Yes, Sweets?" He would try to keep it normal. Perhaps she would open up to him. "You know you can tell me anything."

"I don't know what to do," she said in a quiet, frightened voice. "I think someone is trying to hurt me."

That short statement sent a shiver down his spine and caused him to stumble backwards.

* * *

Felicity was shaken up by the events of the previous night for sure but was determined to not let it deter her.

Even after her talk with Joe, where she'd withheld vital information, like the cameras in her apartment, the day's rehearsals had gone well, but suddenly it hit her. Someone had been inside her unit. Probably on more than one occasion. *And they'd been watching her. Violating her privacy.*

Had they watched her undress? Take a shower? Sleep? The police removed all the cameras but didn't tell her where they'd been placed.

She was rehearsing what was to be her signature song when the realisation hit home. *She could have been attacked. Or worse, killed.*

A shiver went through her, and then she forgot the words.

She *never* forgot her words. Ever.

"Felicity, Sweets," Joe said, concerned. "What's wrong?" He was quickly at her side.

"Nothing," she said, staring down at the floor, and knowing it was a blatant lie. "I just forgot the words." She kicked at the floorboards with her toe.

"My darling, it is obvious something is very wrong," Joe said. "You forgot the words." He reached forward and wiped his fingers across her cheek. "And there are tears," he said sadly. "I thought we'd talked about this issue you're having."

Felicity wiped her own hand across her cheek. There *were* tears. She hadn't even realised; she was so engrossed in her thoughts.

"Oh Joe," she said, stepping into his comforting arms. "It's all such a mess."

"A mess?" Joe looked confused. He had no idea about the chaos that was last night. The full chaos. "Let's sit down and you can tell me all about it."

Joe was always there for her. *Always.*

She should have called him last night. He would have come over and sat with her. Made her feel safe after the police left. She'd endured hours of uniformed police as well as detectives. They'd checked her entire house for more cameras, as well as phone taps.

Felicity mentally slapped herself. Joe would have helped her through her ordeal. He was her best friend.

He put his arm around her shoulders and led her toward her dressing room.

Once seated, Felicity looked at him, tears building in her eyes once again. "It was horrible," she said. Then covered her face with her hands.

"Horrible? Joe sat patiently, waiting until she was ready.

"I had to call the police," she said, looking up briefly and seeing Joe's horrified expression.

He sprang forward and wrapped her in his arms.

"Oh my poor Sweets! Why didn't you tell me before?"

Felicity told him the whole sordid story, and he listened intently.

"This is not at all good," he said, when she'd finished. "We have to do something."

"Like what?" Felicity demanded. It was okay to say it, but what could anyone do?

"I don't know," Joe admitted. "But we'll come up with something," he said quietly. "Stay with Maurice and me tonight?" He looked apologetic, as though he knew it was a lame idea.

She looked at him long and hard. "And let them win? No way," she said, determined. "But thanks anyway."

Joe sighed in resignation. Felicity wondered if she was doing the right thing in turning down his generous offer.

"Back to rehearsals," she said. "I promise not to forget the words this time." With that, she stood and made her way back to the rehearsal room.

* * *

Joe met with Derek after Felicity had left for the day. He had to be told, despite all of Felicity's protests. *It wasn't his problem, it didn't affect him, he didn't need to know*, she'd said. None of it worked. Joe had an obligation to tell Derek about the stalker. Even if he didn't, he would still tell him. Felicity needed to be safe.

Derek was horrified at the news.

Not only was someone harassing her by phone, he was physically stalking Felicity, as well.

"So, you actually saw this guy?" he asked Joe.

"Kind of." Joe was a man of few words unless necessary, which Derek fully appreciated. "I saw a silhouette at the window." Joe shivered. "He bolted when he realised I'd seen him."

Derek sat quietly, considering their options.

"And you're sure it wasn't Hector?" He shook his head, trying to shake that thought away. "Scrap that. Hector wouldn't try to hide his presence. He'd make sure everyone knew it was him."

Joe sat bolt upright and gazed directly into Derek's eyes. "I've known the man for over fifteen years. He's the lowest of the low, but he would not stalk his own daughter. I'm absolutely sure of it." He paused briefly. "He wouldn't want to be found out either. He's a coward of the highest order."

Joe sat contemplating how much to tell Derek, but decided he needed the full story. "The police found hidden cameras in her apartment." It was blunt but needed to be said.

Derek sat upright and rubbed his hands through his hair. "Then there is no option," he said calmly. "I'll organise a body guard to protect her." He sat back, satisfied with the decision he'd made.

Joe sat there, watching Derek, and grinning like a Cheshire Cat.

"What?" Derek asked, puzzled.

Joe chuckled. "You obviously don't know our Felicity as well as you think. She won't agree to that, I'm certain."

Derek opened his mouth to speak but was interrupted.

"Don't get me wrong, I totally agree with that idea. But I know Felicity won't."

Derek sat back into his chair, feeling more than a little frustrated. Sometimes Felicity was too stubborn for her own good.

Chapter Six

It had been a long week of rehearsals. As much as she'd tried to keep things normal, Felicity found herself glancing toward the uncovered windows all the time, making sure no one was out there.

She was becoming paranoid, but that's what happens when someone was invading your entire life.

There had been no phone calls for a few days. It was almost like they knew she had a trace on her phone.

And all had been quiet on the home front. No more items in the wrong places, no more noises or phone calls in the quiet of the night.

Meow was not so skittish, which also indicated things were back to normal. Felicity hoped whoever had been bothering her had finally given up after all this time.

It was almost as though it had never happened. *Almost.*

Felicity had even gotten over her phobia about sleeping in the apartment. At one point she was afraid to go to sleep. In her own apartment no less.

But she'd slept last night. It was now the weekend, and she had slept in. And no rehearsals today.

Felicity slowly opened her eyes to the light surrounding her.

She snuggled under the covers, and didn't want to get out of bed. Meow jumped on the bed as if saying *"Good morning!"* It was probably more like *"Feed me!"* Felicity decided.

"I suppose I have to get up now," she told her beautiful, but impatient cat. But instead snuggled further under the covers and closed her eyes again.

This time Meow jumped on top of Felicity and put her face down close, rubbing her cheek against her owner's face.

"Okay, I'll get up this time." Felicity put one foot out of the covers, then reluctantly slid around and out of bed.

* * *

When Joe arrived at Felicity's apartment he found the front door wide open. That was definitely not like Felicity. And even more unlikely with all this stalker stuff going on.

"Felicity! Sweets!" he called at the top of his voice. "We need to talk."

He stood at the door listening for any movement or sounds of occupation.

Nothing.

If she was home he'd expect something. Anything. A slight shuffle here and there. Not this emptiness. This nothingness.

"Meow," he called out, knowing the dear cat would come running to him if she was around. Again, nothing.

It scared him. Terrified him.

Felicity would never leave the front door wide open like this. She just wouldn't.

He had a momentary thought that Felicity had run away from her problems. Her stalker. But she wouldn't abscond. That just wasn't Felicity. And anyway, if she did that, she certainly wouldn't leave her apartment open for all and sundry to gain entrance.

He shook himself. This was not his Felicity. She faced things head-on. There was no way she'd run. She wanted this. Wanted it so badly. She was working ten or twelve hours a day most of the time, working toward her goal. Her end plan.

A shiver shot down his spine.

Where the heck was she? "Felicity." He called gingerly as he tapped lightly on the door. He knew in his heart she wasn't there and began to walk away.

Her car. Felicity always parked her car in the underground parking reserved for tenants. Slowly, fearfully, he made his way to the underground car park.

Joe hadn't realised he was holding his breath until it all came out in a whoosh when he saw the car, right where it was meant to be. *She was home, she just didn't hear him, no need to panic.*

Making his way back to her apartment, his fears were renewed. Was she ill? Otherwise she would have heard him knock and call out, surely.

Again he tried to rouse her, to no avail.

He resolved to go inside. What else could he do? Felicity may have collapsed and there was no one to help her.

Joe went from room to room, checking out the entire apartment.

"Oh my!" Now Joe was panicking. There was no one home, and no sign of Meow. His concern made his face ache. Made his head hurt and his heart split in two.

His heart was pounding; something was very wrong. He would stake his life on it.

He paced out the front of her unit. He shoved his hands into his pockets, then pulled them out again.

He didn't know what to do. Didn't want to worry anyone, but knew he needed to tell someone. Anyone.

He stood motionless momentarily, considering his options as his heart felt like it was trying to push its way out of his chest. But it was past time for action.

Joe whipped out his phone and called the police. Then he called Derek.

* * *

After the police had been around the other night, Felicity had felt safer. Much safer. She was sure her stalker would give up after that, knowing she was more than willing to call in the police.

But apparently not.

Because here she was, running for her life, clutching poor Meow who was scared to bits. Her darling kitty couldn't understand why she was holding her tightly and running for dear life.

All the buildings were a blur; she ran so fast. Someone was in her apartment.

Again.

And while she was there, no less.

She stifled a sob. *That would not help. Not at all.*

Felicity didn't have a plan of where to go. She just grabbed Meow and ran, hanging on for all she was worth.

She refused to go through the back streets this time. Although it was daylight, she wasn't going to risk being in that dingy alleyway, where anything could happen, and no one would be there to help.

So she took the main route. It meant passing through the tiny shopping strip where there was usually a lot of people around. The bakery was there, as well as the pharmacy.

Perhaps she should just go into one of them? But no, they didn't know her and would probably look at her like she was a mad person when she told her story.

As she raced past the bakery, the aroma of freshly baked bread almost lulled her into a false sense of security. She decided to go in there and ask for help, but saw it was empty of customers. The intruder could easily snatch her if the staff were out the back.

Instead she continued onto her chosen path. She headed for the deli.

George would know what to do. He was a wise man, and her friend. He'd helped her before, and he'd help her again, she was certain.

The deli was close now, just around the corner. It was so close she was sure she could smell the wonderful aromas that always came from George's Deli, no matter the time of day.

Help was within reach; she was almost there. Felicity stiffened. She could hear someone running behind her. Getting closer and closer. She held her breath but didn't dare glance back; she just kept running as fast as she could.

Felicity screamed long and loud as someone touched her shoulder.

"Sorry lady," the young man said as he continued jogging along the lonely street. The look he gave her was priceless. Little did he know what he'd done to her with that one tiny accidental action.

Felicity's heart was racing, her muscles tensed. She was breathing rapidly, gasping for air she knew she didn't need, and her whole body was shaking.

Her lungs burned, and it felt like she would never breathe properly again.

Most of all, she felt faint. She must be hyperventilating. She was nearly there, she couldn't succumb when the end play was so close at hand.

Through all this, she held on tight to Meow.

She staggered the rest of the way to the deli, and when she finally arrived, was on the verge of passing out.

"Felicity!" George was with her in a flash and grabbed her quickly. He stared into her face momentarily. No doubt he could see her trembling chin. She could feel it trembling, but darned if she could stop it.

Tears streamed down her face involuntarily.

"Here! Sit!" he demanded, pulling out a chair for her.

"I, I, I..." She couldn't get any words out.

"It's okay," George said. "Just sit and calm down and we'll work it out." She felt like her legs were crumbling below her, and she thanked her lucky stars for the chair that now held her up. His kindly eyes made her feel at least a little better, and her breath came out in a whoosh.

"Coffee, I think," he said, busying himself at the coffee machine.

Felicity sat back, still clutching Meow who was now purring to his heart's content. She tried to get her breathing under control, but it was taking so long.

Breathe in, 1,2,3. Breathe out, 1,2,3.

She was getting there, slowly but surely.

She wiped her clammy hands on her clothes and began to relax - just a little. It wasn't over, was far from over.

What George was thinking, she had no idea, but the truth would have to come out sooner or later.

George bought two coffees over to her table and sat himself opposite Felicity and Meow. He let her drink her coffee in silence, watching and waiting. Her hands were shaking, and he was watching them closely.

When her breathing was back to normal he patted her hand. "Feeling better?" he asked, a frown on his face.

"Yes, thank you," she said timidly.

George sat patiently waiting, didn't try to force anything from her. *Good old George.*

"I, um," How did you say something like this? "Someone broke into my apartment and was trying to hurt me."

George sat upright. "Oh my goodness!" he almost shouted. "Are you okay? Did they hurt you?" He was now holding her hand tightly. "Who was it?" he demanded.

She swallowed. Hard. "I don't know. He's been stalking me," she whispered, afraid to say it out loud.

George looked shocked, and Felicity watched as his colour faded.

He sat there stony faced for what seemed like forever but would have only been minutes. After an eternity, he gulped down his coffee then stood. He opened his mouth as if to speak but didn't. It was as if he was having second thoughts.

"George?" Felicity said, waiting expectantly.

"We need to call the police," he said blandly.

Felicity felt the blood drain from her face but nodded her agreement.

She knew it was the right thing to do. Someone, her stalker, had gotten into her apartment. Again. She'd grabbed Meow and ran for dear life.

She didn't even stop to lock the door, fearing he would still be there when she got home.

But now, George was using the common sense she wasn't currently capable of using.

She continued to sip her coffee as George made the phone call.

"Yes, she's safe now. She's here at the deli with me."

He hung up the phone and went back to Felicity. "The police will be here soon," he said.

Felicity let out a sigh.

"They're are at your apartment too," he added. "Your friend Joe called them when he found it abandoned."

Felicity sat dumbfounded, not sure what to say. So much trouble over some random lunatic who was stalking her for what reason, she didn't know.

She was still lost in her thoughts when two officers walked into the deli. To her amazement it was the same two officers who came to her apartment a few days ago.

"We meet again," Officer Pete said to her.

"So he's still bothering you," the other officer said matter of factly. "Any ideas about who it might be?"

Felicity shook her head. "None whatsoever." She took a deep breath, trying to keep herself calm. "I saw him this time, if that's any help," she said. "So now I know he's not a figment of my imagination." She put on a quivering smile.

"He was never a figment of your imagination," Pete said, trying to reassure her.

The other cop rubbed his hands together. "Great. I'll get a description from you and we'll also get you to sit with our sketch artist."

Felicity nodded meekly. This was all just too overwhelming. It couldn't be happening. Not to her.

The officer took the description from her and closed his notebook. As he did the door suddenly opened and Joe burst in.

"Sweets! Oh my," he said dramatically but honestly. "I was so very worried."

Felicity saw the tears in his eyes moments before he grabbed her and held her tight.

"Reow!" Poor Meow was in the middle of the hug and was complaining loudly.

Derek arrived only moments later, looking decidedly worried.

Joe grabbed Meow as Derek moved in for a comforting hug.

* * *

With everything else that had occurred recently, Felicity wasn't in a festive mood. According to Joe, she needed to be.

She pulled the artificial Christmas tree from the cupboard and set it up in the sitting room. Meow watched her every move.

The last time she'd put the tree up, she'd found her kitty at the top of the tree just moments before it hit the floor.

That was three years ago – hopefully he was old enough now to leave the decorations and the tree alone.

She pulled tinsel out of the box of decorations. It looked a little tired. Perhaps she should have replaced it this year.

Felicity shrugged her shoulders. What was the point? She rarely had visitors, so she was only person who would see it.

She wouldn't have even bothered except Joe kept asking when she was putting the darned thing up. Besides, she didn't feel at all festive. Especially this year.

She sighed. Joe pushed her to do things she wouldn't normally do. That wasn't necessarily a bad thing. Reaching up to put the angel on top of the tree, Felicity knew he was right – she needed some normality in her life again.

They would get her through this. Joe, Maurice, and Derek; they were her guardian angels.

Draping tinsel around the room, she looked about. No one would have ever guessed she was being stalked, or that she'd been stalked and filmed inside her own apartment.

The thought made her shiver.

* * *

Felicity insisted rehearsals and scheduled performances continued. Derek wasn't thrilled, but finally agreed.

Curtains had been added to all the windows, stalling any attempts for her to be watched from outside.

At first it felt isolating, but Felicity gave herself a good talking to, and shook herself into acceptance. Really, it was no different to having your curtains closed at night. Right?

Of course it was right.

Life wasn't meant to be easy – she'd been reminded of that old saying all through her life, and it was certainly relevant now.

But the show must go on and go on it would.

"And one, two, three, left." Joe's voice urged her to keep practicing the choreographed moves. "One, two, three, right." He let go of her hand. "Now try it on your own." He stepped aside and watched her practice, his hand on his chin in typical Joe style.

Felicity straightened her back and squared her shoulders. She pretended to hold onto her beautiful gown, the one that wasn't there, but would be wearing on performance night.

"And again." His frown told her that Joe wasn't happy with the moves. He watched carefully, then rubbed his hand across his face. "Something isn't right. We need changes, Sweets. Hang on."

Joe turned and walked toward the back of the room where he had a discussion with Maurice. He returned with a pair of stunning stilettos.

Felicity gasped. "I'm wearing those?" She was used to wear high-heeled shoes, but these were a little over the top. "I need to see the dress." It wasn't a demand, it wasn't her being precious, she just needed to know for practicality purposes.

Joe waved Maurice forward. He held a stunning organza dress in his hand. Felicity adored the salmon colour but wasn't so sure about the chunky shoulder straps. And it was short. Very short.

At least it wasn't so long she would trip over the hem in her stilettos. "Okay, but what's with the shoulder straps?" She laughed and lightened the mood.

Maurice breathed a sigh of relief. Felicity wasn't sure why, because she rarely vetoed Maurice's clothing choices. He was good at what he did.

"Let me practice with the shoes." She sat on a nearby chair and put the stunning shoes on. She smiled at Maurice. "Perfect fit." After all these years, Maurice knew her size perfectly.

Felicity was wobbly on her feet, but persisted, and went for a stroll around the room. "Okay, let's give this a whirl."

The music started, and she began the choreographed number, almost twisting her ankle in the process. She waved Joe away as he ran toward her.

Again she persisted. She just needed to get the hang of this. She'd get there, she knew she would.

Slow clapping came from the back of the room. It was Derek. Her heart skipped a beat, and her mood lifted. How long had he been watching her?

She continued with her dance practice, while she belted out the song. As she bowed at the end of the performance, it occurred to her that Derek's presence had lifted her mood. A lot.

Derek strolled slowly toward her. *Did he feel the same way?*

Of course he did. He'd proved it with his actions. She loved being wrapped in his arms, held tight, but not too tight. The warmth from his body enveloped her in love.

She was confused. Not sure it was love, but perhaps just infatuation. That can happen when two people worked closely together like they'd done over these past months.

Felicity felt his presence before she saw him standing next to her. She always had an awareness when he was close by.

She stepped forward and wrapped her arms around him, not saying a word. She didn't need to. He didn't need to. They understood each other, supported in each. They loved each other.

Felicity gasped. *Love? Did Derek love her?* She wasn't sure.

She assumed it was love that she felt toward Derek, but one never really knew. As she clung to him, she sank into his body, savouring his touch, wanting his lips on hers.

"Ahem." She abruptly looked up. Joe stood there, amusement clearly showing on his face.

She frowned. then stepped back out of Derek's embrace. Heat worked its way up her neck, and across her face. She shrank backwards, trying to sneak out of there. But it was too late. Joe knew her too well and laughed.

Not at her, though. He'd never do that. He was making sure she knew how pleased he was that she was finally happy. That she'd found a man who made her happy; someone he was sure wouldn't disappoint her or let her down.

Derek was her forever man. Yep, that's what Joe would be thinking for sure.

Suddenly Derek grabbed her by the hand and pulled her toward her dressing room. She looked at him dubiously. Instead of speaking, he put his finger to his lips and continued his journey. Their journey.

Once they'd entered the make-shift dressing room, Derek closed the door behind them. It was the only spot in the whole warehouse that offered any privacy.

"Let's try again," he whispered into her ear. "Only this time without the onlookers." He watched as Felicity took a steadying breath. She breathed in his cologne. He watched as a smile began, and pulled her to him.

"I love a woman who takes control." Derek felt her jump as he spoke. He'd startled her when he whispered in her ear. His hands were firmly around her waist, and he was breathing in her beautiful scent. Lavender if he wasn't mistaken. His grandmother used to grow it in her garden and make sachets of it each year for Christmas gifts. As a young boy, it was his job to cut the lavender and bring it inside to dry, ready to be packaged. It was a bitter-sweet memory, as they'd lost her some years ago.

Derek shook the memory from his mind. He didn't want to remember this now, only wanted to immerse himself in everything that was Felicity.

Every beautiful crevice, every soft curve, and every elegant movement. When she laughed, a little tinkle escaped her lips, lifting him high every time. But when she was sad or scared, it changed everything.

He ran his hands down her back, then in a circular motion. She was tense, very tense, and he was trying to relieve some of her stress. It was no wonder she was stressed.

He'd told her it was business as usual, and not to worry, but he was certain that would be impossible. Knowing someone wanted you dead was not an everyday occurrence, so he totally understood her position.

Derek's lips found the sensitive spot behind her ear. Felicity leaned backward, almost as though she was trying to get away. "You don't like it?" he asked quietly.

"Oh yes, yes I do," she said. "But everyone out there will know what we're doing." She sounded like she cared. Derek didn't.

He let his hands fall to his side and walked to the door. As he opened it he called out. "Anyone object to me kissing Felicity?" He heard her gasp, and chuckled.

"Nope, no one," Joe called back, amusement in his voice.

Derek closed the door and walked back to Felicity. "I guess that's settled then."

Once again his arms went up around her back, and his lips lightly brushed across her lips. She tasted good. Like pink lemonade on a hot day. Refreshing and making his lips tingle. He'd never experienced anything like it before. "Mmmmm, nice," he said, without even thinking.

He moved closer, and once again her fragrance drifted into his consciousness. He edged closer, leaving little distance between them. His hands moved up to the back of her head and slid through her hair.

"You taste good," he told her, seconds before claiming her lips again. She moved closer, ever so slightly but enough that his senses heightened. Every time she moved, her curves distracted him. When she pushed into him, her breasts rubbed against his chest. It sorely tested his control.

Her hands slipped beneath his suit jacket until there was only the thin material of his shirt between them. The breath hitched in his throat. "Felicity." His voice was barely above a whisper. He gazed down at her. The want in her eyes made his heart break. He took a long, steadying breath.

He leaned down and kissed her again. She was his favourite taste, nothing could compete.

Derek knew he had to stop now. With great difficulty, he pushed himself away.

"Later," he said, straightening his clothes. "I won't turn this into something sleazy." And with that he leaned in for a quick kiss and left the dressing-room with Felicity staring after him.

* * *

As she applied her makeup, Felicity could hear the rumblings of early arrivers.

She was always nervous before a performance, and tonight was no different.

Soft music played in the background, songs she would sing throughout the night – all Blues songs.

It helped calm her nerves somewhat.

Tonight was important. It was opening night. The first night in her new persona. It would be a make or break night in many ways.

Derek had contacted the press, and there would be critics in the audience. Their good reviews were imperative to her future career.

But Felicity tried to put that to the back of her mind. She needed to concentrate on delivering the best performance possible.

Joe came up behind her and placed his hands on her shoulders. She jumped visibly. "Nervous, Sweets?"

"Always," she answered, a smile teetering on her lips.

He tightened his grip. "You'll do well; we both know you will."

She stood and faced him, and Joe wiped away a tiny smudge of mascara, then leaned in and placed a light kiss on her forehead. "Break a leg," he said affectionately. "Now," he said with more force, "Let's get you dolled up." With that he turned toward her waiting wardrobe racks.

Maurice fluttered into the dressing room. It was his job to make sure Felicity was properly attired. "This is your first outfit," he said, grabbing the salmon chiffon off the rack. He leaned forward and snatched up the pair of stilettos he'd shown her during rehearsals. "Paired with these beauties."

Felicity sighed. She hated those over-the-top stilettos, but if she must, she must.

"Thanks Maurice," she said with a smile, but knew he'd see through the façade. He usually did.

"Mwah." Maurice took pride in his work, and the outfits he chose always enhanced her performances.

The two men helped her dress, and the three began to leave the room. They were met by Derek. His eyes went wide.

"Wow, amazing," he said, taking both her hands in his. "You look gorgeous. Stunning." He leaned in for a hug.

"Stop!" Maurice and Joe said in unison.

"You'll crush her dress," Joe finished.

Derek stepped back, duly admonished, a big grin on his face regardless.

* * *

The Etta James hit rolled over her lips with ease.

Felicity was at home on the stage. No wonder her parents had pushed her into a life of performing. Even as a four-year-old, future stardom would have beckoned. A shiver engulfed Derek's body.

He was almost overcome with emotion. Joe tapped him on the shoulder, invading his moment of pride.

"She's amazing." Pride and pure joy were written all over Joe's face. It was clear he'd always known she was destined for greatness.

He watched as Joe swiped at his eyes. "I must have an eyelash in there," he said, a smug smile on his face.

Staying hidden from the audience by the stage curtains, Derek watched as Felicity glanced around the room, watching her audience watching her, as she finished her first song.

The room exploded with applause and she received a standing ovation.

A star had emerged.

"Bravo! Bravo, my darling." Joe was the first person to reach her as she left the stage. He handed her a small posy of flowers, as he always did at the end of her first performance of a tour. "You were amazing."

Felicity took them and hugged him gently. "And you are biased, but thank you," she whispered into his ear. She laughed as she moved back. "You are always so kind."

"Fabulous, fantastic," Derek approached her now. "Amazing." He handed her a single red rose and moved in for a hug. But this hug was not a friendly one like Joe's.

This one was more emotional. Personal. And meant a lot more to the both of them.

She studied the rose. A red rose for love, or just because? Either way, coming from Derek it meant a lot to her.

She studied his face. His eyes were bright, and he was smiling broadly. "Well done!"

She stared at his lips, then licked hers. It was too much for them both, and he leaned down and kissed her ever so lightly.

Felicity leaned closer toward him, savouring the feel of him, loving the heat emanating from his body, and just loving being near him. With him. Tasting him, feeling his lips on hers, ever so gently.

"Ooooh, Felicity!" This time it was Maurice. Like the others, he would want to congratulate her. This was the routine after first performance. In fact, everyone rallied around her after every performance.

Her dear friends understood how uncertain she felt about her performances, how much she lacked the confidence she needed to make it big.

It was comforting to know they were all there, surrounding her with their love.

Chapter Seven

Felicity took a deep breath, and let it out slowly then began to sing.

This was one of her most favourite songs, but one of the hardest to sing. She glanced around the room. This place was so much better than the lowlife dive she had sung in previously.

Thank goodness for Derek St James. The man was a godsend – in many ways.

A low murmur moved across the room. Felicity's eyes scanned the audience as the murmur became a buzz. She tried to ignore it as she continued.

Confusion set in. The audience were looking about, talking to each other, not concentrating on her.

She tried to read their faces but couldn't tell if it was uncertainty or something else.

One thing was sure, she was worried. What the heck was going on? No one was listening to her. Even the orchestra faltered, which was unheard of.

She looked across to the off-stage area where Derek and Joe were standing, watching. They looked worried too.

People began to stand up, still glancing about. Someone was screaming now, and people began running. She turned toward the backstage area again when she heard someone call her name urgently.

"Get down!" It was Maurice. He was waving his hands about, indicating to her to drop to the floor. What the….?

The wind was knocked out of her as someone slammed into her, knocking her to the ground. A stranger lay atop her, pinning her to the stage. Felicity felt his hot breath as he whispered in her ear. "It's okay, I've got you. Stay down until I give the all-clear."

The stranger scrutinised the room as Felicity's confusion deepened. Who was this bear of a man? She struggled beneath him, but to no avail.

As quickly as he pinned her to the floor, he was up and pulling her to her feet. "What…? Who…?" Her words were cut off as she was dragged off stage and into the backstage area.

Derek ran forward, pulling her into his arms. Holding her tightly. Felicity was still confused. What the heck was going on?

Her head was foggy, she couldn't think. "What just happened?" She was in a daze, trying to think through a fog. "Derek?"

Felicity looked down at her beautiful chiffon dress. It was dirty and ripped. Nothing like the gorgeous gown she had donned before stepping out onto the stage.

Her heart beat rapidly. With her hand on Derek's chest, she could feel his heartbeat too. It was thumping in time with hers. This… whatever it was…had affected him as much as it had her.

"Dom, thanks. You're worth your weight in gold." Derek's hand was outstretched toward the stranger who had knocked her to the ground.

"Dom?" *Who was this man? This not-so-gentle giant?* As she scanned him from head to toe, Felicity noticed the gun in his hand. She faltered, and fell backwards, out of Derek's arms.

Dom grabbed her and pushed her toward the back entrance of the building, his urgency evident. Still holding the gun in his hand, he propelled her toward the locked door.

A new level of fear overcame her. She couldn't wrench her eyes away from the gun – the silver glistening in the lights, piercing her memory, hurting her brain.

As she stood, trying to take it all in, the fog surrounding her began to clear. There was screaming in the background, the sound of people running, voices trying to reassure.

She stared at Derek. He was dishevelled, his hair all over the place, his suit skewed, and his normally calm expression was gone.

He ran a hand through his hair, a gesture she'd come to know as an indication of nerves or frustration.

She straightened her back and crossed her arms over her chest. Stood firmly in place. "Right. Now tell me what the heck is going on." No one spoke. The men looked at each other blankly. "Okay, I'm leaving. Alone"

Now they looked shocked. Scared even.

Derek let out a resigned sigh and took her hands. "This is Dom. He's your bodyguard." He held his hand out in front to stop her interrupting. "Someone is trying to kill you." Felicity felt the colour drain from her face. Someone was trying to kill her? Why would they do that? She faltered again. Her knees trembled, and her head spun.

No! She wouldn't faint. She wasn't weak. She wasn't going to let this get the better of her. Felicity shook her head, trying to clear it once more. She clamped her feet to the ground, wriggled her shoulders, and straightened her spine once again.

She released her hands from Derek's and walked toward the stage entrance, glancing into the stadium without revealing herself.

She could feel their gazes burning into her back. They watched her every move. Dom moved closer, but she waved him away. He stood strong, didn't waver for even a moment. He was at her side, and it was obvious that nothing would move him. Not now, and not ever.

That was reassuring.

Felicity stared at the chaos. The bedlam that ensued shocked her. Police were everywhere, audience members, now relatively calm, were being led out the emergency exits. She quickly pulled her head back from the danger zone, taking a deep, steadying breath.

Oh. My. Gosh. This was real. It wasn't a joke, or a dream. It was unnervingly real.

Putting a hand to her chest, she took another gulp of air, trying to still her pounding heart. Felicity felt herself being pulled back into a chair and looked up into Derek's face.

"Wh… why?" That was all she managed to get out. She was reeling from this revelation. Someone wanted her dead. And what's more, they were willing to go through with it.

* * *

Felicity winced as she was tucked in underneath Dom's arm, close to his body.

As he guided her toward the back entrance, beads of sweat moistened her face.

Bedlam was all around her. People shouting, running, police everywhere. Dom told her to keep her head down and not look up. He kept her huddled close to him, with one arm around her, while the other held his gun.

She was close to tears – the stress was unbearable.

Amidst all the madness, she recalled the night Derek waited outside another venue in the back alley for her. The overwhelming darkness amidst unfamiliar noises in the background. Noises that put her on high alert, while, at the same time, feeling she was safe with Derek nearby.

Shadows in the darkness are never a good thing, and now she had to face them again. At least this time she wasn't alone. It didn't stop her heart from beating so hard it felt like it would hurtle out of her chest.

"You're okay, Felicity. Just keep your head down." It was Derek. She felt his hand on her back, trying to reassure her. "We won't let anything happen to you."

It was true. There was no way he would let anyone hurt her. She bit back a sob, wondering why anyone would want to do this to her. She'd never done anything to hurt anyone. Always kept to herself, was a pillar of society, and she sure as heck didn't deserve to be shot at by some deranged stranger.

She jumped as the security door slammed shut behind them. A car waited outside the door, and she was quickly ushered into it. This time she didn't have to face the darkness alone. This time the back entrance was well lit.

Once inside she sat back, sighing with relief.

"It's not over yet." It was Derek again. She'd been placed between Dom and Derek. Obviously for her safety, but it worried her that they'd put their lives on the line for her. She winced at the unfairness of it all.

"Why are they doing this?" Her voice was so quiet, so unnatural she didn't recognise it. Her whole body quivered, and as she stared down into her lap, she noticed the tremors in her hands. Derek reached out and took her hands in his, rubbing his thumb across her palm, trying to ease her stress.

His eyes pinned hers as he answered. "We have no idea. Do you?" His brown eyes pierced her soul, and as much as she tried, she couldn't look away.

"N-no." She was not surprised at the waver of her voice, nor was she surprised at how soft it was. It was not every day someone tried to end your life.

Derek lifted her hand to his lips. "We need to find out why this is happening, so it can be stopped."

The car began to slow. They must be at their destination. "Where are we?" Felicity gazed around. She didn't recognise this place at all.

This time Dom spoke. "You'll be safe here. No one knows about this location." His voice held no emotion. He'd probably done this so many times before that it would be an everyday occurrence. Felicity stared at the gun sitting across his lap.

"Do you really need that thing?" The last word came out with disdain. She hated guns with a vengeance. And she sure didn't want it to be anywhere near her.

"I'm afraid so. It's needed to keep you safe." Felicity scrutinised his face. It was probably the first time she'd really seen him. There was too much panic and mayhem earlier. Too much chaos and confusion.

She sighed again. It seemed like everything was out of her hands. Control had been tossed out the window.

Would her life ever be normal again?

* * *

"I don't understand. Any of it." Derek sat next to her on the comfortable sofa in their isolated hideaway. "Why does someone want me dead?"

Felicity stifled a sob and fought back tears that had been threatening to escape for several hours, since that fateful moment when Dom knocked her to the ground. "I've never hurt a soul. Not ever." She was more than distraught, and if she wasn't careful, she could quickly become a sobbing mess.

"I know." Derek's voice was low and comforting. "The police are trying to find out, but so far they've learned nothing." Frustration gave an edge to his voice. She understood completely because she felt it too.

"They did learn something of concern though."

Felicity heard herself gasp. She was shocked, of course she was. She'd lived a fairly placid life, had never broken the law, and certainly hadn't done anything that would make someone want to murder her.

Derek waved his hands in front of his face. "No, no. Not about you. It's nothing you've done." Her shoulders sagged in relief.

"It's Hector. He…"

"What has he done now?" Her hackles rose. He had been the bane of her life for as long as she could remember. If he wasn't her father, she'd have broken all ties with him years ago. Probably should have done it anyway.

"Gambling."

She felt her face go tight. She was frowning, she knew she was. She slid to the edge of the sofa, waiting for Derek to continue.

"He owes some bad people a lot of money."

Jumping to her feet she paced the floor before she could even think about it. "And so someone tries to kill me because my father owes them money?" She fisted her hands and held them tight against her body. "That is so not fair. I didn't do anything to them. Or him." She clenched her fists. "That low-life. He did this to me. Just like he's done so many other things to ruin my life. I'm sure he hates me."

"Well, to be fair," Derek said, looking everywhere except at her, "We're not positive that's the reason, but it's all we've found so far."

Slumping back on to the sofa she put her hands to her face. This time she let the tears flow. She needed to get Hector Montgomery out of her system, and out of her life. Forever.

* * *

She'd had her cry, and hopefully that was the end of it. But Felicity was still really cross.

No! Angry. Furious even, at her father. How dare he put her life in danger! All for the sake of his stupid gambling habit.

Did her mother know what he'd been up to? Probably not – they'd hardly spoken for years. Felicity still saw her mother, but things weren't great between them. She'd always believed her mother was as much to blame for all the anguish she'd endured over the years at the hands of her father.

She'd let him bully her.

She'd let him push her into the music industry as a toddler.

And she'd sure as heck let him take her money. Greedily grasping all of it.

For her sake, he'd said. He'd bought her a house. But it wasn't in her name. Hector was the legal owner of it.

He'd bought her a car. Again, in Hector's name.

She owned her little unit, but only because she'd refused to allow Hector to handle any of her money once she turned 18.

Oh sure, he said he was her manager. Raved and ranted about all he had done for her. How ungrateful she was. She would be a nobody if it hadn't been for him. On and on he had gone for about five minutes. When the abuse didn't work, he had threatened her. They had no written contract, so she had defied him, obtained legal advice and told him straight.

He wasn't her manager, and he never would be again.

She'd watched him closely as they'd argued. He wasn't upset that their working relationship had ended. Wasn't sad or remorseful for what he'd done. He was *enraged* because he would never get his hands on her money again.

He continued to coach her for a fee, to 'guide her toward stardom' he said, but Felicity knew better. Fame meant more money, and Hector wanted as much of it as he could get his greedy hands on.

Not happening. Not now, and not ever again.

She'd finally broken those unrelenting ties.

She sat with her eyes closed and took a deep restorative breath. Keeping calm was going to be difficult. Being so angry was not at all good for her well-being.

Well neither was being shot at! She hadn't asked for this, hadn't done a thing to cause it. *Breath. Breath. Calm. Breath. Breath. Calm. Breath. Breath. Calm.*

Slowly she opened her eyes, only to discover Derek watching her every move. No doubt wondering what she would do next.

"I'm okay," she said, moving to a standing position. "I'm forcing myself to be calm. To not be so *angry*." The last word came out forceful, and ironically, angry.

"It's not working, then?" Derek asked, a chuckle escaping his lips. She glared at him.

"Not funny." Now she was pouting. She didn't do pouting. Okay, yes she did, but usually when she didn't get her own way. And usually when Hector was involved.

Hector! Her blood pressure moved upward again, so taking a deep breath she slowly let it out.

Derek watched her. Closely watched her. "I'm okay." His expression told her he didn't believe it. "Really. This time I really am okay."

"Good, because you can't let him get the better of you."

He was totally right. Her father had done so much to ruin her life, but this time he wouldn't win. She would make sure of it.

* * *

Derek had insisted it wasn't safe for Felicity to go home, so she'd been staying at a hotel.

The hotel was dressed ready for the festive season. A large Christmas tree stood in the foyer. Decorations were strewn all around the walls.

Even the room was decorated for the upcoming season.

Everywhere she went, Dom went too. He was there around the clock, even when his side-kick was on duty.

The hotel was wonderful, luxurious even, but it wasn't home.

Felicity had adored the spa in her luxury room, and had used it several times, soaking her weary body in the enormous tub, adding loads of scent-filled bubble-bath.

She missed Meow.

They'd only been there a few days, and he was being looked after, but she still missed him.

Finally, Derek took her back to his place, giving her a break from the monotony of the hotel. At least his place wasn't dressed up with Christmas decorations.

It just felt so inappropriate right now.

From the moment she stepped inside his mansion, Felicity was in awe of her surroundings. The hotel had nothing on this place. You only had to look at the clothes Derek wore to know he was a man of money, but now she was blown away.

The entrance reminded her of a historical movie with its spiral staircase with a beautiful woman gliding down the stairs. This was the height of luxury, and so far, she hadn't gone beyond the front door.

His living room alone was bigger than her entire apartment.

"Sit. Take a load off." He motioned toward the black leather lounge suite that stood just inside the door.

Felicity surveyed the room. Everything was perfectly co-ordinated. In addition to the lounge suite, there were several recliners, all black, to match the sofa. Each chair had a matching ottoman, and it all sat on expensive beige carpet.

As she sat, Felicity stared at the far wall, with its floor to ceiling windows. The view across the bay was amazing. She couldn't wait to see it once the sun went down.

Derek was one lucky man. She'd thought perhaps he'd come into money but knew deep down it was hard work that got him where he was today.

But with no one to share it with, what was the point? At least in her tiny apartment she was happy, and she had Meow. She was such a loveable cat, and it was always a thrill to be welcomed home by her each night.

Meow. She'd tried not to think about the kitty, because she missed her so very much.

"What's up?" Derek's voice came out of nowhere, and she startled.

"I was thinking about Meow." She watched as he contemplated her, sitting down beside her as he did. "I miss her."

"She's okay. She's being cared for." She must have looked as if she didn't believe him because he added, "I promise."

She nodded slowly and sank back into the luxurious sofa. It was a certainty she could lose herself in this thing.

Derek's hand reached out and he touched her cheek. Softly but with so much passion. He leaned in and his lips touched hers ever so gently. Like fairies dancing across her lips. She sighed, wanting more. Needing more.

She wondered if Dom hadn't been standing nearby would the kiss have been so chaste.

Felicity was running. She had to get away, but this place was unfamiliar, and she had no idea where to go.

She stole a glance behind her, trying to catch a glimpse of this person who wanted to kill her. What she saw terrified her. He was tall, really tall, and he was built like a bear. He was running, trying to catch up with her, and Felicity knew for sure he would eventually reach her. His long legs meant that his one step would equal two of hers; it was inevitable that she would be outrun.

She took a deep breath, endeavoring to keep herself from running out of air when she needed it most.

As she turned the corner, she slammed into something hard. It was him. But how could he be around the corner when he was behind her? Felicity was totally confused now. She closed her eyes momentarily and shook her head trying to clear the fog in her brain. She opened her eyes. Wide. And stared at the man blocking her escape.

"What....?" She was more confused than before. This man was definitely the same man chasing after her.

He grabbed her by the shoulders and began to shake her. "Felicity." She felt his grip on her shoulders. "Felicity, wake up."

She opened her eyes and stared into Derek's concerned eyes. She sighed. Deeply. Thank goodness it was only a nightmare. But it was so incredibly real.

"You were screaming, like, really screaming. What happened?" He appeared really concerned, as she knew he would be.

Felicity leaned into him, and put her arms around Derek, holding him tightly. She felt the tears trickle down her face. "It was so real. I was there, and he was chasing…." Derek put a finger to her lips.

"I will not let anyone hurt you. Ever. I promise." His hand came up and massaged her back, trying to help her relax. She felt safe here, felt safe with Derek. And she was certain he'd keep her from harm.

Now all they had to do was find out who was trying to kill her, and why.

Chapter Eight

Dom was there. Always there. Even as she slept.

She slept in the bedroom while he was next door in the lounge room. She'd insisted – how could she sleep knowing his eyes were on her every movement?

This had been the routine for about a week now. They would come home from performances, and Dom would thoroughly check out the luxury hotel apartment while Derek stood with her at the door.

It was surreal.

As Dom checked out the apartment, she glared at the stunning Christmas decorations strewn around her room. If she could, she'd have them all removed.

It felt further from Christmas than she ever imagined possible.

Besides, Felicity was tired of it all. She wanted to go home. Her real home, where Meow would cuddle up with her while she read her novel, then snuggle in once she turned off the light.

She really missed Meow. A lot. She stifled a sob. Joe and Maurice were caring for her dear kitty, and truth be known, spoiling her rotten.

They had their own spoiled feline – Cfer. It meant C for Cat they'd told her when their own kitty had arrived many years ago. They are usually very serious on the surface, but once you got to know the pair, you saw a totally different side to them.

Tonight's performance put Felicity on edge. Derek had arranged for some of the country's top critics to be in the audience. They could literally make or break her career. It was that vital.

She'd given it her best, but she feared her best would not be good enough. Derek assured her it was the absolute best performance to date.

But he would say that.

Even if it was the worst, he would still tell her it was her best. She knew he would.

Security had been high since the attempt on her life. Dom was with her every moment until she went on stage. Then he was standing in the curtains, as close to her as he could get. There were two dozen security officers placed around the room, including many in plain clothes. She felt safe and secure, thanks to Dom and Derek.

She was still reeling from tonight's show, and very hyped up. It was high paced as usual, and her brain went into overload. It always took several hours for her to come down from that natural high she got from performing in front of an audience.

She'd sat with Dom and Derek for a couple of hours and talked. About anything and everything. She knew she was animated but couldn't help it. That's just what she was like when a show was over.

Finally, she'd calmed down and finally gone to bed. Derek had gone home, and Dom had taken up his usual position in the lounge room.

He'd rearranged the furniture the day they arrived so he could hear any movement in her bedroom. But they were on the third floor. How could anyone get in, except via the front door?

Felicity finally closed her novel and turned off the bedside lamp.

The bed was so luxurious, and she snuggled down into it. It was like having a holiday at a deluxe resort.

But it was way quieter here. There were no tourists to disturb your peace and quiet, no babies crying, and no children running up and down the passageway.

Major win.

Felicity glanced across at the beside clock. 2am – time for some shuteye.

She closed her eyes, and quickly drifted into a deep sleep.

Unsure what had woken her, Felicity looked around the darkened room. A tiny stream of light escaped though a small gap in the curtains. The bedside clock told her it was 4.30am – not quite daybreak.

She closed her eyes and tried to get back to sleep.

She suddenly opened her eyes again. What was that sound?

She glanced around. It was pitch black, she couldn't see a thing, but sensed someone in the room.

Would Dom have come in to check on her while she slept? Felicity didn't think so.

She rolled over in an effort to get a better look without being obvious. This time she saw the silhouette of a man.

A big man.

Big as a bear.

Like she'd seen in her apartment. Her first thought was how did he get in?

Her next thought was on how to get help. Should she shout for Dom? Scream? Jump out of bed?

Her eyes hit the bright light of the bedside clock. Without further thought, she suddenly reached out from the bedding and swept the bedside clock from the table. She hoped it landed hard enough for Dom to hear it. The massive silhouette moved toward her, hands outreached.

She jumped out of bed as Dom rushed thought the door, flicking on the light as he did so.

Gun in hand, he yelled "Freeze, scumbag." Ignoring Dom, the persistent intruder continued on his path toward Felicity. "Last warning," Dom yelled. "I *will* use this gun."

The intruder laughed. Felicity was frozen to the spot. Everything seemed to slow down around her.

She saw the man dive toward her. Dom subsequently moved to her. He shoved her aside, putting himself between her and the low-life who had invaded her room.

"Don't move!" Dom was angry now, she could tell, but he was still totally in control.

It all happened in a blur, but she clearly remembered hearing the gunshot, then her ears were ringing.

The intruder was down, and Dom was helping her off the floor and leading her into the other room, and out of harm's way.

Then he was on the phone, his gun still trained on the injured man. First with the police, then hotel security, and last of all, Derek.

Her heart was racing. She felt shaky, and when she looked down, saw she was visibly shaking. Whether that was fear, shock, or adrenalin, she didn't know.

What she did know was she was eternally grateful for Dom. If he hadn't been there…

She didn't want to think about it. She closed her eyes momentarily and was surprised when they began to leak. Dom threw her a blanket. "Here, put this around yourself," he said. "I think you're in shock.

Was she? She wasn't sure but did what he said. In the next instant, police and security burst through the door. The intruder was handcuffed and ordered to stay on the floor until the ambulance arrived. When they finally came, Dom asked them to check

Felicity out first, but because the intruder was bleeding, he got priority, much to Dom's disgust.

Amidst all the confusion, the hotel doctor arrived and checked Felicity over.

Everything had happened so quickly, and she was having trouble getting her head around it all. Derek was suddenly next to her, wrapping her in a long embrace, and holding her tight.

"Thank the Lord for Dom," he muttered, as he continued to hold her firmly. She was quietly sobbing, and he began to rock her gently, while still keeping her encased in his strong arms.

She looked up into his face. "You look terrible," she told him, and he laughed.

She joined him but continued to laugh until she cried.

This was crazy. The whole night was crazy.

The doctor told Derek she was in shock, and she conceded she probably was. She felt the blanket being pulled up around her again. "I'm alright," she heard herself say as she stood, but her voice sounded like it was far away.

"No, she's not," Derek told the doctor, and before she knew what was happening, she felt herself slowly slide to the ground. Even as she discovered she was laying on an ambulance stretcher, she was still protesting. "I'm alright," she said again, to no avail.

* * *

It was over.

She had her life back again. They'd caught the stalker, the man who had nearly ruined her life.

The person who wanted her dead.

Felicity breathed a long sigh of relief. She didn't have to worry about her stalker again.

Dom had shot him, but he would be okay. So much so, he'd spend many years in jail, paying for what he had done to her. The realisation that her father was not responsible was a huge relief. Perhaps he really did love her after all. She'd always thought he did, in his own twisted way.

She kept replaying over and over in her mind, how the stalker had tried to kill her. His hands were outstretched, trying to get to her throat. He was going to choke her to death. No one seemed to know why he'd become obsessed with her, but he had.

Why would *she* have a crazed fan? She wasn't famous, far from it. And hardly anyone knew about her. Except maybe her fans. Finally, the penny dropped. She *did* have fans. Lots of them.

As she lay in the hospital bed, Derek by her side, she tried not to think about the night's events. Putting them out of her mind was difficult.

Derek squeezed her hand. It was as though he could read her thoughts. He lifted her hand to his lips and kissed it. "A penny for your thoughts," he said.

"I'll need more than a penny," she answered. "They are beyond horrible." She shuddered.

A nurse came in and took her blood pressure. "Doctor will be here shortly, and then you can go home," she said.

* * *

After everything that had happened over the past months and days, Felicity realized life truly was short.

She could easily have died in that hotel room. If it hadn't been for Dom intervening, James Muldoon, her stalker, could easily have maimed her. Or murdered her. She shuddered just thinking about it. Finally, after days of recovering, Felicity felt she was back to normal. Not that everyone agreed, but she couldn't let Muldoon take over her life.

It had all been a wake up call for her. She had been in denial over many things, but especially over her feelings for Derek. She had tried to stifle those feelings because they were in a working relationship.

So what if they were? Why did it matter? She admonished herself for not admitting the truth when they first met.

She resolved to finally give into her true feelings for Derek, and not delay the inevitable any longer. But how did she tell him? She was certain he felt the same way, although he'd never put it into words either. They made a good pair. Both cowards when it came to love.

Christmas was fast approaching, and Felicity had been doing some shopping when she walked past a music store. Something about the song made her stop where she stood. She drifted into the store for a better listen. It didn't take long, but in that moment, she knew what she had to do to ensure a lifetime with the love of her life, Derek St James.

* * *

"Can you stop fussing?" The question was aimed at Joe, who was standing in her dressing room, fretting over every little thing.

He threw his hands in the air. "I was just trying to help," he said as he pouted.

She smiled at his reflection in the mirror. "Okay fuss-pot," she said, "Keep going then."

Joe was fixing her hair. Not that Felicity needed help, she was more than capable of doing her own hair and make-up; she'd been doing them for a very long time. But Felicity knew why he was worrying. Tonight's performance was very special. Not only because it was her last performance before Christmas, but because they'd added an extra song to the regular show.

It would be the last song for the night but was not listed on the program. This song was special and meant more to her than anything she'd ever sung before.

Finally, ready to perform, Felicity realized the irony of tonight's song list. Most of the songs she performed each night were love songs. Or songs about losing someone. And some were about the pitfalls of being in love.

She took a deep breath and began to walk out onto the stage to a peal of applause. Felicity surveyed the room. Tonight was a record crowd. Even the private boxes were full. She breathed in again, then out, trying to steady her heartbeat. She was feeling a little agitated tonight, and she knew the reason. This meant so much more to her than a normal performance. This performance could, and hopefully would, change her entire life.

As she left the backstage area, Joe called out to her. "Break a leg," he said, as he blew an air-kiss her way.

Derek had learned by now that hugs were not allowed when she was in stage attire, and also blew an air-kiss, but his had much more meaning.

As she slowly walked down the dreaded on-stage stairs, Felicity felt a film of sweat on her face. *She never perspired on stage. What was wrong with her?*

She felt as though she was jerking as she walked. She glanced across at Maurice – he would have his eyes on her and wondering what was going on. She put her hands to her chest and took a deep calming breath before she began to sing.

Rapid applause began with her first words, but it didn't help with her concern. Sweat continued to trickle down her neck. Felicity knew what was going on. She was changing the routine and didn't know if it would come across badly. Especially with Derek.

She had practiced the routine with Joe many times. He had choreographed it, and Maurice had chosen an outfit that she would need to change into quickly. They'd been careful to keep it secret from Derek.

The first song was over and was a huge success. If the audience had picked up on her state of mind, they didn't show it.

This was her first standing ovation of the evening, and hopefully wouldn't be her last.

She took three steps backwards and two to the left, which would get her to the bottom of the stairs she'd come down during her entrance.

For this song she was to stand on the bottom step, resting one arm on the rail. She looked up, waiting for her music cue, and began to sing an Etta James song. The words were strong and clear, and people were standing and applauding. This had to be her best audience to date.

After three more songs, there was a short break and Felicity changed her outfit and freshened up, as she did during each performance.

"Wow, best performance ever!" Derek said, more than a little pleased. He kissed her cheek as she reapplied her make-up. Felicity was fanning herself with a pile of papers. "Hot?" Derek asked, as he reached for some cold water, and handed it to her. She only took a few sips, then handed it back.

"Thanks. I'm fine," she said. "It's a little warm in here today." Derek frowned. It wasn't hot, and she knew it. Derek knew it too. It was all on her. She was anxious about what was to come.

Maurice came in with her next ensemble. It was a soft pink chiffon number, with a sheer mesh beaded back. It flowed beautifully all the way to the floor, and when she put it on, it looked absolutely stunning. This was Felicity's favourite of all the outfits she wore during this show. And the way Derek looked at her when she wore it she guessed it was his too. She slipped on the matching shoes moments before leaving the room to return to the stage.

The lights slowly went down, which was her cue to be ready. The orchestra would begin playing and Felicity would enter the stage. One of her favourite songs was next.

She looked across at Derek and tears began to well in her eyes. She needed to pull herself together, be professional and get through the night without faltering. Not even once.

After another succession of songs, Felicity was more than half way through the program. She was now on the last stint, and the lights lowered as she left the stage.

Felicity went back to her dressing room and freshened up once more, and with that came another dress change.

She had nearly reached her main target. "You're sure the orchestra know?" Felicity asked Joe, concerned it would all fall in a heap.

"They know. Stop stressing, Sweets. It's all under control." Maurice brought in her outfit, and it was almost time to return to the stage for the last time tonight. Except for that song.

This time she was singing a soft and romantic song that she loved. Then came another romantic song and it was nearly the end of the show.

When her last song was over, Felicity left the stage. Now was usually the time for her standing ovation. She would normally leave the stage and come back on, take another bow, and then she'd leave. But tonight was different. She would leave the stage, do a quick outfit change, then come back on and sing her heart out, hoping it was enough. Her heart thudded.

Would it work?

She wouldn't know until after her final performance.

Maurice had chosen something special for her very last song. The one that mattered so much to her. It was deep burgundy in colour and had wide shoulder straps. The dress was tight fitting and was clearly made to entice. The neckline was low, with a silky underlay, and chiffon on top. The bodice was covered in intricate beading that went all the way past the hips and into the thigh area. It then flared out to a mermaid style at the floor. It had tiny buttons at the back. Tiny enough to frustrate a man in a hurry.

As she left the stage, Maurice and Joe pulled her aside and undressed her. They hurriedly put the dress on her, fastening the buttons as quickly as humanly possible. Joe fiddled with her hair and reapplied her dark red lipstick, while she put on the shiny black stilettos.

The applause was loud and clear. It. Was. Time.

Felicity stepped out from behind the curtain to find Derek waiting there. Confusion was written all over his face. "What's going on?" he asked, as she walked straight past him. He turned to Joe but got no response. Instead, Joe hooked his arm through Derek's and led him to the edge of the stage.

Felicity's hands were clammy. She had no idea how Derek was going to react. The orchestra played the lead-in, and she waited for her cue, keeping her eyes to the audience. She licked her lips, nerves getting the better of her, then slowly turned her head toward Derek.

She began to sing *All I Want for Christmas is You* to him, and him alone, then walked across the stage. Taking Derek's hand, she pulled him onto the stage. She could feel the tears welling up in her eyes, but she had to get through the song. At the end, she asked Derek to marry her. In front of the entire audience.

 The crowd roared. There was a standing ovation and the applause continued for over five minutes. Joe and Maurice bought flowers onto the stage for Felicity and shook Derek's hand then hugged him. They were so happy for Felicity and were ecstatic for the two lovebirds.

Felicity wrapped her arms around Derek's neck and kissed him, causing the audience to go into uproar all over again. Cameras were flashing, people were whistling and shouting, and Felicity was crying. Truth be known, Derek was too. She was sure she saw a tear or two there.

Christmas would be wonderful after all.

Epilogue

Derek looked back toward the entrance to the packed chapel. And toward Felicity.

His future wife. The love of his life.

She wore an A-line knee length white dress. It was strapless with a lace bodice that continued half way down the top layer of the dress. It appeared to have a silk lining with at least two layers of chiffon. She wore matching silk stilettos. No doubt Maurice had a hand in choosing her wedding outfit. Derek grinned – he knew Felicity would have groaned at the stilettos being introduced.

She wore a tiny white hat on the side of her head, ditching the traditional wedding veil. Chiffon had been creatively attached, along with some silk flowers. Trust Maurice to coordinate everything beautifully.

Felicity stood tall, both her arms hooked with Joe's on one side and Maurice's on the other. They'd been more like fathers to her than her own disgraceful father.

Derek looked into her face and she winked at him. She was so beautiful, but today she was beyond beautiful. She was totally stunning.

The wedding march began, and quiet took over the large chapel. The three began to walk slowly down the aisle, then halted. Joe and Maurice glanced around, and Joe kissed Felicity's cheek before unhooking her arm. Then the two men stepped back.

Random people began to stand up. Guests appeared confused. Heck, Derek was confused, what was going on?

They nodded their heads as though acknowledging each other, then lifted their instruments and began to play. Derek suddenly realized those standing were members of Felicity's orchestra. He looked toward her again. She tapped her feet, and seemly out of nowhere, lifted a microphone to her mouth and began to gyrate her body. Everyone began to clap and cheer. Derek stood there totally dumbfounded as she began to sing.

Her voice was strong and clear. Even today she wouldn't falter. She was a total professional.

He felt a grin cross his face. He should have known those three would pull a stunt like this.

The guests were all having a wonderful time, and frankly, so was he. Joe caught his eye and gave him the thumbs up. Derek returned the favour and Joe winked at him. Maurice just stood there with a big grin on his face.

As Felicity worked her way down the aisle and around the perimeter of the chapel, she never missed a beat. Her carefully choreographed performance was flawless.

Even at her own wedding she was the ultimate professional.

Cameras clicked and flashed, but she didn't flinch, not even once.

For the final chorus, she worked her way toward Derek who was grinning like a Cheshire cat, he was sure. He was so happy, and surprisingly felt totally relaxed. His feet were tapping, and his heart was full of happiness. All he wanted now was to marry the woman he loved.

Felicity received a standing ovation for her performance, as she should. Best performance yet. She indicated to the orchestra to receive their own accolades. Duly deserved, Derek decided. They were totally out of their comfort zone, fabulous, and professional.

The song now finished, Joe and Maurice made their way toward the altar. Felicity took her place next to Derek, and the minister moved in to his designated position.

"Who gives this woman away?" he asked.

"We do," Joe and Maurice said in unison. Derek was certain he saw a tear slide down Joe's face.

Most of the ceremony was lost on Derek. He was too busy watching his soon-to-be wife.

"I now pronounce you man and wife." It was all Derek was waiting for. He scooped up his new bride and kissed her passionately, not worrying about the congregation, then strolled down the aisle, still carrying her. He was never one for formalities and wasn't about to start now.

The minute the newly married couple were outside, confetti and rice were thrown their way. Derek gently place Felicity on the ground, putting his hand around her back and protecting her fiercely. After all she'd been through, he wasn't letting her out of his sight.

Dom was there too – as an invited guest. He had saved Felicity's life, after all. He'd since become a dear friend and was very protective of her.

As they walked toward the waiting car, friends and family surrounding them, Felicity leaned in and whispered in her new husband's ear. "I love you, Derek. You are my forever man," she said, as she wiped a tear from her cheek.

* * *

Three years later

Derek and Felicity sat side by side at the news conference, five-month-old baby Alicia cradled on her mother's knee. It was her first media conference since their baby was born.

"Is this end of your career?" a reporter shouted.

Felicity rolled her eyes. "Why would you think that? I had a baby, not a heart transplant." She turned to Derek. If they weren't in front of television cameras with microphones everywhere, she would have whispered a few things to him.

Along the lines of what kind of fools do we have here?

Cameras flashed and Felicity covered Alicia's eyes. "I specifically said no flash. If it happens again, we're leaving," she said in no uncertain terms.

A little under four years ago, Felicity had no idea how far she could come in such a relatively short period of time.

Derek had been right all along – she was now considered a super-star. But not because she wore slinky nearly-there costumes, but for her voice. No men ogled her on stage, and her father wasn't a constant burden or source of stress to her.

Since Alicia was born, she'd seen her parents several times. Despite everything, she wouldn't deny her parents the right to see their grandchild.

It was going to take a long time but she was trying to mend the rift between them.

"Felicity," the reported shouted. "Will there be more children?"

She turned to Derek and grinned. "That's inevitable," she said, glancing across at her husband who was now grinning.

"One last question." She looked to the television reporter. "Will your children be groomed for the industry as you were?"

That made Felicity pause. Did she want her children going through what she did? She licked her lips. "My children will be allowed to be children. If they decide to work in the industry when they are older, that will be their choice." She paused to let that sink in. "So no, they won't be groomed."

"That's all. Thanks for coming everyone."

Derek reached out and took Alicia, and Felicity stood, showing off her most recent baby bump.

Cameras flashed and mumbling could be heard throughout the room.

She grinned as she glanced across at her husband, then at Joe and Maurice standing to the side. She lamented the fact none of this would have been possible if the three most important men in her life had not ganged up on her that fateful day three years ago.

From the Author

Thank you so much for reading my book – I hope you enjoyed it.

I would greatly appreciate you leaving a review, even if it is only a one-liner. It helps to have my books more visible!

Other contemporary Christmas romances you may enjoy are:

The Christmas Proposal

Her Christmas Surprise

About the Author

Multi-published, award-winning and bestselling author Cheryl Wright, former secretary, debt collector, account manager, writing coach, and shopping tour hostess, loves reading.

She writes both historical romantic suspense, and historical western romance.

Cheryl lives in Melbourne, Australia, and is married with two adult children and has six grandchildren, and twin great-grandchildren.

When she's not writing, she can be found in her craft room making greeting cards.

Links

Website: *http://www.cheryl-wright.com/*

Facebook Reader Group:
https://www.facebook.com/groups/cherylwrightauthor/

Join My Newsletter:
https://cheryl-wright.com/newsletter/
(and receive a free book)